THE STORY OF
ANNA AND THE KING

THE STORY OF
ANNA AND THE KING

A BOOK BY CECELIA HOLLAND

A HarperEntertainment Book
from HarperPerennial

HarperEntertainment books may be purchased for educational, business, or sales promotional use. For information please write: Special Markets Department, HarperCollins Publishers Inc., 10 East 53rd Street, New York, NY 10022-5299.

FIRST EDITION

Designed by Jeannette Jacobs

Library of Congress Cataloging-in-Publication Data is available.

ISBN 0-06-107372-5
00 01 02 03 04 10 9 8 7 6 5 4 3 2 1

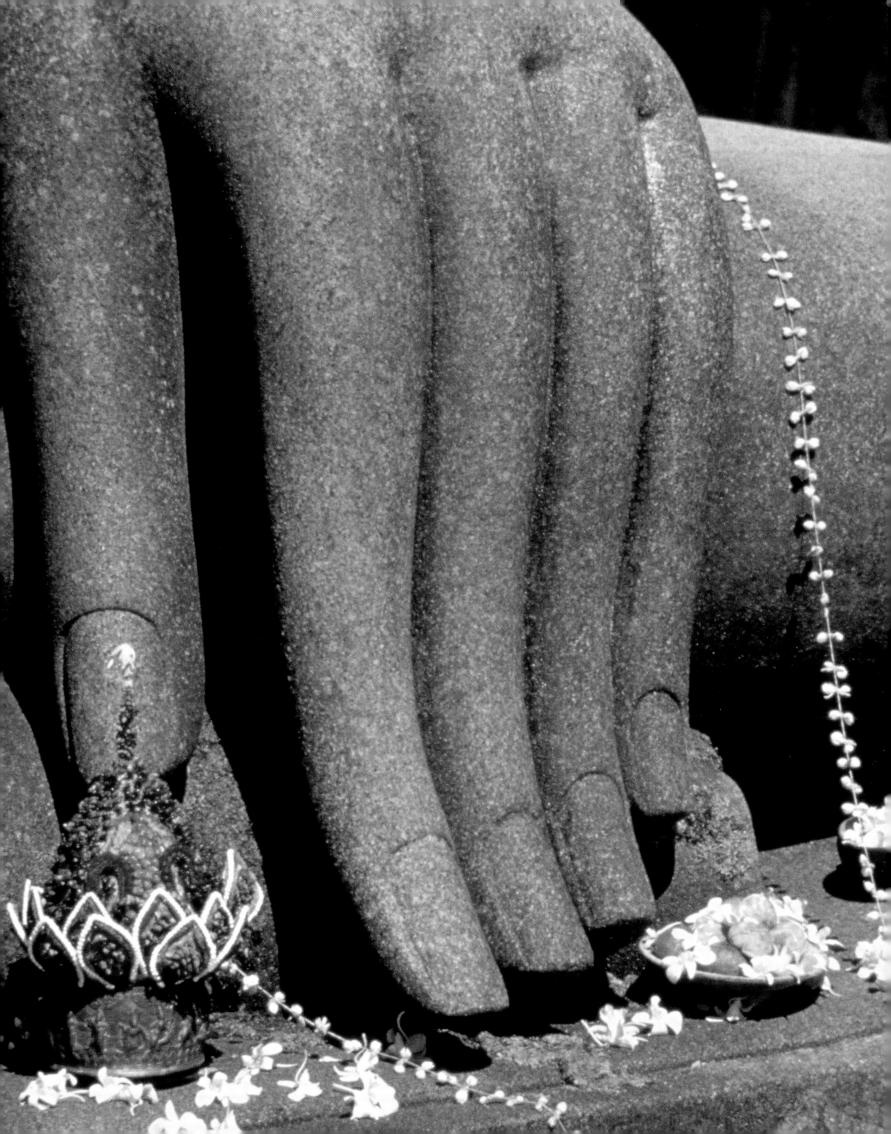

One day early in the making of *Anna and the King*, director Andy Tennant walked down a busy Bangkok street and into his own movie.

The day was already hot, the street filled with busy people, the hubbub of traffic, and the colorful clutter of shops and displays. There, alongside the hurrying crowd, some actors were putting on a street opera. Tennant, stopping to watch, quickly found himself one of a swelling crowd of onlookers. The exuberant performance was dazzling in red and gold costumes and bursts of music and the extravagant gestures of the actors. The crowd erupted in cheers and applause and whoops of laughter. Caught up in this impromptu celebration of the joy of life, the American director felt his movie come alive around him.

He knew right then what he wanted to do with *Anna and the King*: to capture that excitement, that zest and fire, that overflowing profusion of color and image and feeling, that sheer delight in life that is the heart of Thai and make it the backdrop and setting for the legendary story of the governess and the king.

To bring this vision into being, Twentieth-Century Fox would rebuild part of the nineteenth century. Assemble a cast and crew from all over the world. Turn ten miles of cloth into intricate and magnificent costumes. Recruit hundreds of animal actors, from elephants to a crocodile. Battle giant snakes and the blazing tropical sun. And take a beloved story and reinvent it as an epic for the next century as it has been a beacon for this one.

Anna and the King is the real-life story of Anna Leonowens—a young English widow who in 1862 went to Siam to teach English to the children of the king. Her adventure has set imaginations on fire since its inception, in her own books, a novel, a

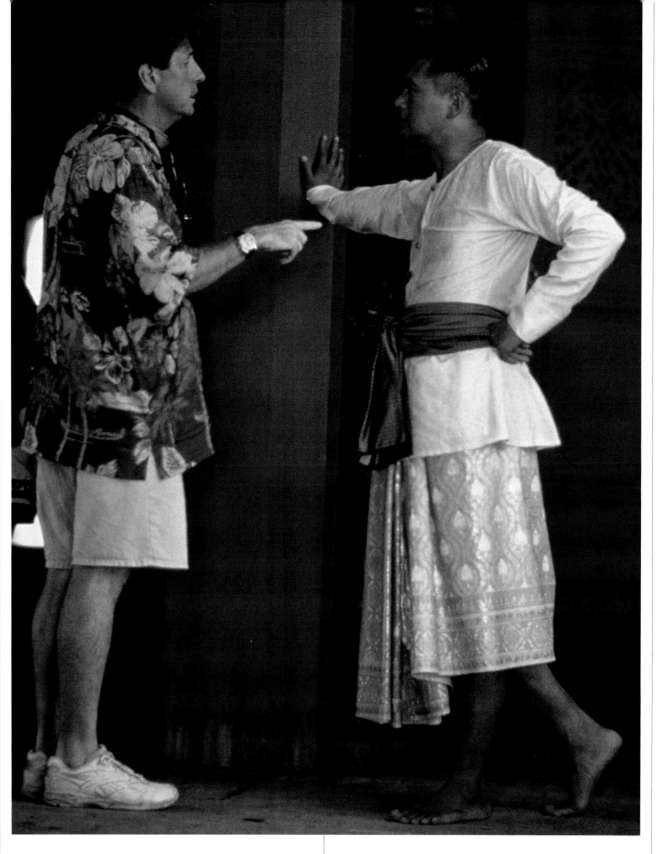

film, and then the smash-hit Rodgers and Hammerstein stage musical *The King and I*, which also became one of the most celebrated motion pictures of all time.

Yet the story has never been completely told. Andy Tennant and Fox knew that the only way to bring this splendid epic alive was to film it in steaming Southeast Asia—lush and mysterious, thrilling and charming, ancient and always new. It must be told with a fresh face, on a huge scale, as epic as the adventure it was for Anna and for King Mongkut, each on the brink of a new world.

For the role of Anna Leonowens, the young widow and mother whose adventure changed the world, there was only one possible star: Jodie Foster, the most brilliant actress of her generation, whose fiercely independent intelligence and serene and timeless beauty are a match for Anna's own. With the story at last opened out to its true scope, Jodie plays Anna as the heroic woman and mother who set forward into an unknown world with no weapons but her wits and her sense of truth.

Opposite her, as King Mongkut, is Chow Yun-Fat, the Asian superstar, whose virility and charisma bring this greatest of Thai kings brilliantly to life—as absolute monarch, lord and master of a nation, a man worshipped almost as a god—and as a man who finds himself falling in love with the one woman he cannot have.

For these splendid actors Fox made possible a world in which to act. On a golf course hacked out of the jungle in tropical Malaysia, construction crews re-created the Grand Palace of the Supreme King of Siam as it looked in King Mongkut's day: complete with the Palace Gateway, the Temple of the Emerald Buddha, the King's Study, Anna's

Notes, sketches, photographs, doodles—all pieces of the single vast design that will become this magnificent film.

Co-producer Jon Jashni
in the midst of the
beginnings of his movie.

House, and a dozen other places in the sprawling royal complex. Another feature of the set was the jetty, made to dock Mongkut's Royal Barge, a 150-foot dragon boat painted Chinese red and powered by fifty oarsmen.

Every detail of this setting had to be authentic. Oscar-winning production designer Luciana Arrighi studied old photographs and diaries and visited the modern (and modernized) Grand Palace a dozen times, soaking up ambience, steeping herself in the colors and sounds, and noting the smallest items of the design. Thai advisers supervised every aspect of the construction.

"There is a tremendous responsibility that goes along with re-creating something as sacred as the King's Palace," Andy Tennant says. "We made it our priority to be true and respectful to the Thai people and their extraordinary design talents." In fact, the

Behind a snapboard, a
busy street scene begins
to come into focus in the
hazy tropic dawn.

OPPOSITE PAGE:
Director of Photography
Caleb Deschanel rides a
crane to a high shot.

An elephant takes a well-deserved shower after work. Every elephant working in Anna and the King *had his or her own mahout, or groom, to tend to the elephant's needs.*

OPPOSITE PAGE: *A painter adds a final touch to the prow of Mongkut's Royal Barge. Dragons are good luck symbols to the Siamese.*

splendid re-creation of the Grand Palace is a testimony both to the brilliance of Thai culture and to the filmmakers' commitment to presenting it faithfully.

Costume designer Jenny Beavan worked closely with Arrighi to coordinate colors and styles, and to give the film its supreme elegance. She, too, spent months researching, looking for fabric, studying old photographs and books, and finding that Thai fashion, far from changelessly traditional, had its trends. "The Thai fashions in 1862 were eccentric and derivative," she says. "They were influenced by neighboring India as well as China. The French fashions from surrounding colonized territories came into play. A dash of Louis XIV style is seen in the wide selection of hats."

Another of Beavan's responsibilities was creating a wardrobe for the nineteen elephants featured in the film. The elephants were only part of an extensive animal cast that included oxen and chickens, snakes, a man-eating crocodile, and one hundred horses. Famed animal consultant Rona Brown supervised the care and training of these cast members; among her huge crew were seven people whose only job was preparing the elephants' diet of sugarcane, papayas, bananas, hay, and shrubbery.

These giant actors were the largest gathering of elephants ever seen in Malaysia. They came from all over the country, some from zoos and some from an elephant sanctuary. Many were working animals—prized members of Malay logging families—

OPPOSITE PAGE:
The magnificent four-elephant wagon-in-the-making—a masterpiece of the teeming exuberance that characterizes Siamese life and gives such style and excitement to the film.

An artist works on the great stone Buddha of Nong Khai, to whose protection King Mongkut leads his children.

FOLLOWING PAGE:
To design the sets, Luciana Arrighi used watercolor sketches to bring this complex mixture of cultures into clear focus. Here, Anna's stateroom on the Newcastle is her last taste of Victorian comfort before she sets off into unknown and exotic Siam.

and lived in the native family compound and were passed down lovingly from father to son. While on the set of *Anna and the King* they were treated like royalty themselves, and they responded with some wonderful work.

The elephants had a society of their own, as well as strong personalities whose expressions kept things loud and lively in their compound. The intricate workings of the elephant social order fascinated all the crew, especially Jodie Foster. The star spent much of her free time down at the elephant compound, enjoying these great and wonderful beasts, whose work contributes so mightily to the exotic grandeur of the film.

Yet all this is only background to the true spectacle of *Anna and the King*. In the end, the magnificence of this stunning film lies not in the ten miles of cloth, the nineteen elephants with their personal crew of fifty-seven, or even the splendid Grand Palace with its jeweled entrances and tiled floors. The power of this movie is in the story itself, with its sweeping vision of the clash between East and West, between power and love, and between a woman with a great heart and a man with a great vision.

In the splendor of its original setting, with these superb stars in their most ambitious roles, *Anna and the King* unfolds as a story of the universal human struggle to transcend the boundaries of birth and culture in order to reach a common ground of tolerance and love. It is a story for all of us, and for all time.

ANNA IN HER STATEROOM
IN THE NEWCASTLE

THE BRITISH EMPIRE
*Superpower of the
Nineteenth Century*

The story begins with Anna Leonowens, standing on the deck of a ship in the teeming harbor of Bangkok, about to step into another world.

She had left behind the glory of the British Empire, in 1862 the greatest power in history. Queen Victoria was in seclusion after the death of her beloved Prince Albert, but the power of her little island realm now stretched around the globe. The empire lived on trade. Its colonies produced a steady flow of raw materials to the mother country, and England shipped out a steady flow of manufactured goods to the colonies. With major holdings in Africa, China, and the Americas (as well as its crown jewel, the fabulously wealthy subcontinent of India), this gigantic web of empire had grown like a hydra.

It was backed by an enormous war machine: the British Empire had the mightiest navy on the seas; her armies had beaten Napoleon. And her government was dedicated to giving its merchants every advantage in business. Always hungry for more colonies, more markets, more raw materials, and more money, Queen Victoria's empire seemed on a course to devour the world.

In 1857, the bloody Sepoy Mutiny against the Raj in India had shaken up the British system but had not

Jodie Foster as Anna Leonowens—a young widow and mother determined to make her own way in the world—and facing the challenge of a lifetime.

Bangkok Harbor as it must have looked in 1862—with clipper ships and sampans, blazing in the tropical sun.

stopped it. Even after the uprising of native soldiers revealed the supposedly invincible redcoats to be merely human, the superior technology and organization of European armies guaranteed their victory over any forces they might meet in Asia.

Thailand, then called Siam, was in the jaws of a tightening vise. As Anna stood on the dock in Bangkok, her ears ringing with the screams of Siamese boatmen and her awed gaze taking in the splendid pagodas and broad red rooflines of the Royal Palace on the shore, the British were conquering Burma to the north and contemplating the seizure of a number of the Muslim states of the Malay peninsula to the south. Even China had cracked like a nut under the British hammer.

Nor was Britain the only problem facing Thailand. The other European powers had secured colonies, too—although none as extensive as those of Britain. To the east lay the Thais' ancient rival, Cambodia, for which possession the Thai were engaged in a long-drawn-out struggle with Vietnam. But even as the Thai and the Vietnamese made their war talk and marched their armies back and forth, the French were swarming into the Mekong Delta and taking over. The Vietnamese could not match the French firepower; they were sure to fall. Alone of the native states in Southeast Asia, the Thai remained free, but their freedom was precarious, and the Kingdom's course unclear. Anna Leonowens was stepping not only into a strange and exotic country, but into the heart of the clash between East and West.

AN INDEPENDENT WOMAN
The Real Anna Leonowens

The real Anna Leonowens was far more interesting even than the character she invented for herself in her books. Born in India, the daughter of a British infantryman and an Anglo-Indian woman, she grew up an "army rat," living in a barracks with her parents and her older sister, Eliza, in the dusty British garrison town of Ahmednugger. Her father died before she was born and her mother remarried again almost at once, to another soldier in the same garrison.

LEFT: *Tom Selton plays Louis Leonowens, here in typical English Victorian schoolboy garb.*

RIGHT: *In taking up the King's offer to teach his children, Anna Leonowens was leaving behind everything she knew and depended on and was moving into a strange world and an unknown future–and her courage would change Siam forever.*

Life in the barracks was loud and crude and harsh. Only a thin screen divided the little corner where Anna and her family lived from the great noisy common room of the unmarried soldiers. The girls didn't even have beds of their own—they slept on straw ticks on the floor under their parents' bed. When the soldiers were out on patrol, boys could sometimes get permission to sleep in the empty beds, but girls, never.

Growing up, Anna and her sister helped their mother clean, do laundry, and cook, knowing that at age fifteen, they would be thrown out of the barracks to live on their own—unless they married soldiers and set up housekeeping in another corner of the barracks.

Girls like Anna and her sister Eliza were trapped into the same lives their parents had led. They could have no expectations of any decent life outside the barracks; they couldn't even find jobs in the homes of the upper-crust British officers. (No proper Victorian lady would take a servant from such an "immoral" background.) The girls had only one chance to escape this kind of life. Six days out of every week, they went to school.

Anna loved her books, which transported her

out of her squalid childhood and into the dreams and romance of history. She had a quick, subtle mind and a superb gift of self-expression, and she put the education she got at the little garrison school to good use all over the world, whether teaching or writing or lecturing.

But that future lay far off. For now, her fifteenth birthday loomed, and the matter of how she was going to take care of herself became steadily more pressing.

Her elder sister, Eliza, was absorbed into the semislavery of the garrison life. At fifteen she was married to a soldier more than twice her age and went to live with him in another barracks. But Anna rebelled. She had a mind of her own, and she wanted a life of her own, too. Not only intelligent, she was attractive, growing into a striking, exotic beauty with dark eyes and curly dark hair.

Victorian society of the time allowed women neither lives nor minds of their own. Its conventions channeled men and women into narrow and well-defined roles. The men were supposed to be strong, silent, unemotional, capable, bravely bearing the duty God had given Englishmen, that of "civilizing" the rest of the planet (known as the "white man's burden"). Shackled to their sense of superiority, Victorian men sacrificed themselves for Queen and Country, the glory of the Empire, and the stiff upper lip.

Women sacrificed themselves with less fanfare. Conventional wisdom held that a proper Victorian woman was too sensitive and emotional for much contact with the real world. She needed a man to protect her and shield her from the hurly-burly. And if she didn't want that protection, society was quite ready to shove it down her throat. At one point, lawmakers in England even considered making it illegal for a woman to walk alone on a public street.

The sphere in which the proper Victorian woman shone, supposedly, was her own home.

There she was the "angel of the house." Selflessly devoted to her family, she filled their home lives with serenity and goodness, her every moment directed to the benefit of others. She took upon herself every care, duty, and responsibility so that her family would thrive. A central party of her duty and responsibility, of course, was adding to that family, year after year. To get that home and that family, she needed a man.

Anna had no use for that kind of life. She had seen the reality of the angel of the house in her poor, work-worn mother washing laundry in a basin beneath the 110-degree summer sun of India. And she hated the man her stepfather insisted that she marry. By this time she was already in love with someone else, a young clerk in the military pay office. But because her stepfather urged her to take one of his friends instead, she ran away to Malaysia with a missionary when she was fourteen. The missionary taught her Persian and Arabic and history while they spread the Word of God among the Malay. After four years, Anna returned to India.

At once, her stepfather, who had no way of supporting her, tried again to force her into marriage with a friend of his, but Anna, now of age, defied him and married her first love, the pay clerk, Thomas Leon Owens.

Thomas, who eventually changed his name to Thomas Leonowens, became a Brevet-Major, but he never made a good home for his family. He dragged them all over the world, from Southeast Asia to Australia to London and back again to Singapore. Anna probably didn't mind much: She loved new places, strange sights and people, and she picked up languages as naturally as breathing. But in 1859 Thomas died in Singapore (of heat stroke or a heart attack), and he left her with two young children and only her wits to support them all.

Fortunately Anna had excellent wits.

Her daughter was five, her son a year younger. She could have remarried almost at once. Instead,

MURALS

PAINTED SHUTTERS

ON CORNE

COLLECTI OF B AND BOX AND VASES

NY LCQUER JD HER-OF- RL NETS.

LECTION VASES + FLOWERS INCENSE.

> GILT ES JDS ERS LATIVE RINGS

LATTICE DECORATIO ON DADO

she decided to make her own way and took a position teaching in a local garrison school, much like the one where she had learned to read and write and to love books.

For two years she struggled along barely making ends meet. But opportunity was about to knock. Among her pupils were the children of William Adamson, who managed the Singapore office of the Borneo Company. He had spent some time in Bangkok, where he had come to know King Mongkut. When he learned that the King was seeking an English governess to teach his wives and children, he recommended Anna Leonowens at once.

Her friends were horrified. They told her that Thailand—then Siam—was a barbaric country, full of tropical diseases and mysterious, brutal people. She would be mad to go. She would die of some ghastly illness—or worse—be locked up in the King's harem! A proper Victorian angel

would have fainted away at the very suggestion.

Anna, of course, leaped at the chance. She made quick preparations. She interviewed with Adamson and confirmed the British manager's high estimation of her ability. Then she met with the Siamese consul, who was also impressed. Then came a letter from King Mongkut himself.

Unbeknownst to Anna, she was not the first teacher of English Mongkut had brought in for his family. Two American missionary women had taught some of his wives for a time, but these women had been so zealous in their Christianizing that the King threw them out in horror and banned them from the palace.

Therefore, he insisted in his letter that, although she was to teach English, she was not "to convert the scholars." He would give her $100 a month (she would battle with him through her six years in Siam for a raise), and "a brick house in the nearest vicinity to this palace," but she was not to

Another of the set-designer's watercolors shows the plan for the Kralahome's office: compare with the final shot to see how the film grows organically out of the creative imaginations of many people.

Mano Maniam plays the role of Moonshee, the crotchety Muslim husband of Louis's Indian nanny Beebe.

Anna confronts the Kralahome, the King's most powerful minister, in his magnificent office, lavishly decorated with Thai art.

proselytize. She was to teach English, and that only. Anna had no inclinations toward missionary work and agreed to the King's conditions at once.

But she could not take little Avis—not into a harem. Louis, who was six years old now, was still too young to be away from his mother, but by Victorian standards, Avis (at the mature age of seven) was old enough to attend school in England. And so Anna packed up her daughter and shipped her half the world away. Then, with little Louis by the hand and her servants Moonshee and Beebe behind her, she set off for Siam to teach in the harem of the King and arrived in Bangkok.

Before long a showy gondola, fashioned like a dragon, with flashing torches and many paddles, *approached; and a Siamese official mounted the side, swaying himself with an absolute air. The red lan-goutee, or skirt, loosely folded around his person, did not reach his ankles; and to cover his audacious chest and shoulders he had only his own brown polished skin. He was followed by a dozen attendants, who, the moment they stepped from the gangway, sprawled on the deck like huge toads, doubling their arms and legs under them, and pressing their noses against the boards, as if intent on making themselves small by degrees and hideously less. Every Asiatic on deck, coolies and all, prostrates himself, except my two ser-vants, who are bewildered. Moonshee covertly mum-bles his five prayers . . . and Beebe shrinks, and draws her veil of spotted muslin jealously over her charms.*

So Anna Leonowens describes her first meeting with a Thai—the Kralahome, or Prime Minister. Her adventure had begun.

From the beginning, Anna made waves. A single woman, she was expecting condescension from the autocratic Oriental men, and she reacted to every imagined slight with more outrage, more insistence, and more demands. The Thais, of course, saw things a little differently. What she thought of as standing up for her rights they saw as overbearing rudeness. When she stood on her dignity with the Kralahome, at that very first meeting, insisting on being taken to the "brick house" she had been promised, he snorted, turned on his heel, and left her standing there on the deck of the ship, aghast, for an hour or more, wondering what she was going to do next.

At length he sent someone to take her in. The Thais, after all, were a generous and tolerant people. Brought to court for her first reception with the King, she trampled again on Thai etiquette by walking up ahead of all the other people waiting for audience and taking the King on face-to-face. This led to one of the most famous confrontations in film.

"Who? Who? Who?" The King strode toward her, pointing at her with an imperious finger.

Everyone around her dropped to the floor. Anna braced herself; she performed a deep curtsey, her heart hammering. In an echoing silence, surrounded by the bowed backs of people prostrated on the floor, she heard her name and Louis's name pronounced. Stiff with panic, she looked up at the King, who was marching up and down in front of her. His feet were encased in gold slippers glittering with little jewels.

Suddenly he wheeled toward her. "How old shall you be?"

Anna's jaw dropped open; she had not imagined this. The prying into her personal life annoyed her—and she knew that Oriental people revered old age. She said, "One hundred and fifty years old, your Majesty."

Now it was the King's turn to look startled. He resumed his march, looking her over from head to toe, and then abruptly he said, "In what year were you borned?"

She made a quick calculation. "I was born in 1712, your Majesty."

The King's eyes widened. He looked her over again, and fired off another volley. "How many years shall you be married?"

"For several years, your Majesty." Anna was beginning to enjoy herself.

So, obviously, was Mongkut. His black eyes snapping, he pounced. "Then how many grandchildren shall you have by now? How many? How many?" Triumphant, he began to laugh outright, and all around him, the bowed backs of his courtiers shook with mirth. Anna was accepted—if not totally as she hoped to be.

Before long she was going every day into the harem of the King, the Nang Harm, a vast enclosed city inhabited entirely by women. The guards, called the Amazons, were women, as were all the servants; women alone worked in all the shops in the streets of the harem city, and none but women lived in the elegant little houses—with the exception of the young boys living with their mothers.

The King had hundreds of wives. Thai nobles traditionally cemented their bond with their King and assured his favor by sending him a young daughter of the family for his harem. Through these marriages the King was related to every important family in the realm. These women all lived very well: each of the King's wives had her own home, her own servants, her own allowance. Their houses were decked with intricately carved teak furniture, golden ornaments, and curtains and screens of finest silk. But for most of them, it was a life spent in empty and hopeless waiting. Most of the wives never saw Mongkut, or saw him only at a distance.

He had his favorites, some of whom bore him two or three children, and he was, to them, something of a faithful husband. When Anna arrived in Bangkok, he had sixty-seven children by these women, all born since 1851—averaging over six children a year.

As the King said, he was making up for lost time.

Anna saw everything filtered through her Victorian sensibility. Although she had no interest in trying to convert her Thai students to Christianity, she had very definite ideas about justice and equality. From her first moments in Siam she was on a mission to bring Western notions of freedom and law to her new pupils, and to anybody else within reach.

She offended many people because she did not understand the Thai culture, misconstruing motives and reasons. Yet she came to love Siam; that and her great and good heart redeemed her. She did nothing for herself. She saw injustice all around her, and she knew what it meant to be disdained—to be scorned and pushed aside and sold into marriage against one's will. She could not see such deeds done without protest—without, in fact, flying to the King, to the Kralahome, or to anybody who would listen and from whom she could demand justice.

The King was patient with this. When she rose up in mighty indignation about slavery, for instance, he listened to her passionate sermon on the evils of human ownership, and then gave her a copy of the Thai slave laws, pointing out to her the ways in which a slave could earn his freedom. When she sprang to the defense of one of his wives she believed to be ill-used, he replied that every one of the women in the harem, save those who had borne him children, was free to go home if she wished, but none ever had.

The King was growing to like Anna, in spite of what he considered to be her impetuous and outrageous unwomanly ways. His children loved her,

King Mongkut leads Anna into his world.

Tuptim arrives in the palace in a magnificent sedan chair. Every surface is encrusted with images of good fortune and prosperity.

which brought her much to his attention; she was in the palace every day, and the children brought him endless tales of her classroom. Mongkut, we know, loved to talk to foreigners, and took no interest in pomp and ceremony when it did not serve his needs; it's easy to imagine that he came to enjoy his discussions with the eloquent and well-read schoolteacher with the beautiful eyes, who was so quickly shocked and impressed.

Yet it was really the children who brought them together. There was Chulalongkorn, the King's oldest son (although not his heir—not yet). Grave and handsome, the boy loved to study. After a short, sharp measuring of each other, he and Louis became fast friends—a friendship that would last all their lives. Mongkut, too, came to love the brave, clever, high-spirited Louis.

There was Prince Krita, son of the Lady Son Klin (whose name means "Hidden Perfume"). Lady Son Klin was herself one of Anna's most forward pupils, and she undertook to translate *Uncle Tom's Cabin* into Thai, thereby weaving Harriett Beecher Stowe's spirited antislavery novel into the heart of *Anna and the King*.

There was Fa-Ying, the King's favorite little daughter, who preferred drawing to studying Sanskrit. Everybody loved this beautiful child and her adorable quick laugh and love of life. In the jeweled splendor of the palace she seemed herself a living jewel, radiant and delightful. But the year after Anna arrived, cholera swept through Bangkok, and pretty little Fa-Ying fell ill and died. The whole palace was stunned—Anna especially, and the King totally.

"Bitterly," Anna wrote, he "bewailed his darling, calling her by such tender, touching epithets as the lips of loving Christian mothers use. What could I say? What could I do but weep with him?"

Soon after, the King made Anna a Thai noble, gave her the title of Chao Khun Kru (Lord Most Excellent Teacher), and presented her with an

estate. He valued this teacher who gave his children such gifts and whose warmth and loving heart had opened even to him.

Being a Thai noble did not divert her from her one-woman crusade to reform Thai society. In fact, she had a certain power, and the Thai knew it better than she did. As time went on, people desperate to reach the King with some petition or plea tried to

Bai Ling as Tuptim, beautiful and brave, who struggles for a life of her own and dies for it.

get Anna to press it for them. This put her in some danger. Other members of the court, jealous or even fearful of her access to the King, murmured against her. Twice, armed gangs of men attacked her servants in the street; once the King's own guards had to break up such an assault. Other Thai courtiers conspired against her behind her back.

Even Mongkut sometimes lost his temper with her. Once he told her, "Mem, you are one great difficulty. I have much pleasure and favor on you, but you are too obstinate. You are not wise, wherefore are you so difficult? You are only a woman. It is very bad you can be so strongheaded."

Nonetheless, she continued. A beaten slave, an unhappy wife, a mistreated child—all drew her honest outrage. But she respected the one boundary Mongkut had set for her. She had made friends with the American missionaries in Bangkok, and they constantly wheedled her to use her position to spread the light of Christianity over the royal family, but she refused.

Anna, more than the missionaries, sympathized with the Thai. She knew something of Buddhism, and privately shared many of its beliefs. Certainly she understood that the gentle, compassionate, and reassuring ways of Buddha had more appeal to the Thai than the hellfire and damnation of Christianity. In fact, throughout their long careers there, although they brought in many a secular Western blessing, the American missionaries did not convert a single Thai to their faith.

Anna's work was more effective. By means of her English lessons and her cornucopia of stories, she was reaching the Thai princes and princesses, especially Chulalongkorn, with her beliefs about equality and the dignity of all men. The greatest idea of the Western world entered Thailand through the harem school—through Anna Leonowens's patient, persistent teaching. But she would not know this for many years.

Nothing slowed her down—until she got cholera and nearly died. As she lay in her sickbed

The children's park in the Golden Pavilion becomes the beautiful site for Anna's school.

suffering the horrors of the savage disease, her servants weeping around her, a messenger came from the King to promise her that if she lost her battle with the sickness, she need not fear for Louis, because the King would raise her son "as his own."

Perhaps this inspired her almost immediate recovery.

Anna was more and more concerned about Louis. He was growing up in a harem, for one thing, and she saw by his thoughts, his speech, and his values that he was turning into a Thai. Perhaps the time had come to do something about him. The cholera left her drained and weak, so she decided to go to England to improve her health and see her daughter, Avis, again. There she made arrangements for Louis to go to a British boarding school, where he would be molded into a proper little English boy. Why this woman who defied all convention should have wanted conventional children is one of motherhood's mysteries.

The King was reluctant to let her go. The children wept. Prince Chulalongkorn gave her an elaborate good-bye letter, written on stiffened silk and carried in a velvet pouch. With it he included a picture of himself and a present of money. The King gave Louis a present of $100—an extravagant sum—"to buy candy on the voyage," and then suddenly turned to Anna and bade her return soon.

"It shall be," he said, "because you must be a good and true lady. I am often angry with you, and lose my temper, though I have large respect for you. But nevertheless you ought to know you are difficult woman, and more difficult than generality. But you will forget, and come back to my service, for I have more confidence in you every day." Turning on his heel, he walked away across the quay, back to his jeweled and silken palanquin, to be carried back to his palace.

Anna never saw him again.

SIAM

The Golden Land of Southeast Asia

Southeast Asia was the homeland of an ancient culture long before the Thai peoples arrived. The lush and beautiful southeastern corner of Asia nurtured one of the cradles of human civilization. Just as the Nile, the Euphrates and Tigris, and the Huang Ho Rivers made fertile ground for early cultures to grow in, great rivers in the land south of China and east of India also supported prehistoric agricultural communities. The Mae Nem Chao Phraya, or The Great Mother River, runs through the heart of what is now Thailand.

The people of this area were using the local supplies of tin and copper to make bronze for centuries before such technology appeared in the Fertile Crescent and China. They domesticated jungle fowl into chickens and learned to use the labor of water buffalo and elephants. Before anyone else they were cultivating rice. This abundance gave them goods to trade, which brought them riches and ideas, but it also drew invaders, greedy for that wealth.

The land itself is mountainous, with long steep ridges of highland running roughly north-south down from the eastern wedge of the Himalayas. Out of these same mountains stream the many rivers that make boat travel easy, and from earliest times the area was part of the great trading system that included Malaysia, China, India, and the shores beyond. Offering tin, teak, and rice for the goods of foreign lands, Southeast Asians dealt also in the rich ebb and flow of ideas—the art and literature and religious dreams of half the world.

The Thais were relative latecomers to this area. By the time they arrived, the jungle had already overtaken the great temples of Funan, and the towers of Angkor Wat were falling. Hindu princes ruled

Anna crosses a private courtyard in the Grand Palace in the vast, lush tropical night.

in the maritime cities. Sri Lankan monks had brought Theravada Buddhism into the area in the eighth century A.D., four centuries before the Thai came, and the culture was a rich mix of the multiplying Hindu imagination and the daily observance of Buddhist rites and ethics. There was no conflict between the two great faiths; a shrine to the Hindu God Brahma could stand beside a Buddhist wat, or temple, and a man might be a yellow-robed monk one day and God-King the next. The two ideas wove together like the waters of the Chao Phraya.

The people who became the Thai originated to the north, in Yunnan, a province of China, where they had been wetland rice farmers who called themselves the Tai. The Tai were not Chinese. Imperial China maintained a buffer state against them, and this buffer state, Nanchao, kept up enough pressure on the Tai clans that many of them migrated southward, into the mountain valleys and highlands bordering the decaying Khmer Empire in Cambodia.

Then, in the thirteenth century the Mongols invaded south China. Kubulai Khan's armies swept through Nanchao, and the Tai had the choice of becoming the next victims or getting out of the way. They moved south in droves.

Some went to Burma, some to what is now Laos; many went down into the ripe valley of the Chao Phraya, with its brilliant flowers, its birds as bright as its flowers, and its damp soil that could be flooded every year—perfect for growing wetland rice. There, on the ruins of a Khmer outpost, they formed the first of their Kingdoms, Sukhothai, and now this group of the Tai took the new name of Thai, or Free People.

From the beginning the axis of Thai society was the monarchy. To the Thai, their King was the wheel-rolling prince at the center of the universe, whose merit and example kept the whole world turning. He was the earthly manifestation of the *devaraja*, the God-King who ruled the eternal

world. Until King Mongkut, no Thai was permitted to look upon the face of his monarch. The King was absolute master of all his Kingdom, the soul of his people, whom he kept peaceful and prosperous by his right actions. They repaid him with complete devotion and obedience. The ordinary people, the *phrai*, owed him their labor for six months out of every year, to build his houses and forts and walls and canals, and to serve in his armies. Whatever he did was law.

Rich and well led, Thailand prospered.

Tuptim's tragic secret shines through the bride's beauty.

OPPOSITE PAGE: *Tuptim awaits the King in the gleaming silken elegance of the wedding chamber.*

Its armies of infantry, horsemen, and war elephants controlled the petty princes of Cambodia and Laos, and the excellent Thai navy helped extend the power of the Kingdom down the Malay peninsula, and northward through Burma toward India.

In 1433, a fleet of Chinese junks sailed into the Chao Phraya, bringing the greetings of the Emperor of the Central Country to the King at Ayutthaya. The towering oceangoing junks, each holding hundreds of men must have awed the Thai a little as they lay at anchor on the river like great wooden islands. Certainly, when they sailed away, the Chinese took with them the graceful recognition by the Thai monarch that the Chinese Emperor was his overlord. Behind, they left the first of the Chinese merchants who would quickly come to dominate the trade of Thailand.

The next guests came from the opposite direction. In 1497 the Portuguese sailor Vasco da Gama sailed around the Cape of Good Hope and into the Indian Ocean.

Change began slowly. The first of the Europeans to contact the Thai were the Portuguese, who conducted a trading treaty with them in 1516; Ayutthaya was having difficulties with a resurgent Burma and may have paid little attention to the importunate strangers with the round eyes, long noses, and pale skins. In the beginning it must have seemed the Europeans could easily be managed, just as the Thai managed the sizable number of Chinese who ran the internal trade of the country, and who seldom presented any problem to the King.

Toward the end of the century, the Dutch negotiated a deal similar to that of the Portuguese with the Thai King for the rice trade. But in the seven-

A watercolor of the children's pond.

OPPOSITE PAGE: *Some of the King's wives, in the glowing peacock colors of Thai silk.*

teenth century, despite the efforts of the Thai to control their demanding foreign visitors, trouble began.

The Dutch chafed under the original treaty, which restricted prices and the goods they could sell. When the King refused to renegotiate, the Dutch used gunships to force a new treaty on him. The King turned to the French for help. The French built him a new city and fortifications, solving one problem, but they brought with them another: a crowd of zealous Christian missionaries, stoked with the personal interest of King Louis XIV himself.

The preachings and conversions of these French priests aroused the animosity of the Buddhists. The Christians were far less tolerant than the Buddhist church, or *sangha*; they insisted on preaching that all faiths but their own were evil and misguided. But they made converts. The heir to the throne himself became a Christian. Then the old King died.

But there would be no Christian King of Thailand. One of the generals led a violent uprising that killed the Christian prince and many of the missionaries. A fleet of British warships suddenly appeared in the Chao Phraya, which set off another Thai massacre of foreigners. The general who sparked the revolution seized the throne and sent all the foreigners packing; he shut Thailand's doors to the rest of the world for the next 150 years.

In this time of isolation, the richness of the country, the wealth of the farms, and the brilliance of the people combined to blossom into a golden age of literature, art, and wisdom. Ayutthaya was magnificent, with richly ornamented buildings and great temples, libraries full of books, and halls where learned men debated the meanings of the great scriptures.

Yet the outside world it tried to ignore would not stay at a distance. Ancient enemy Burma especially took advantage of the Thais' isolation. In 1767, during one of the many Thai succession

Anna's students, the
King's children, beauti-
ful in their silks and
bangles and their smiles.
Many of Anna's princely
pupils grew up to serve
in the government
and help their
brother Chulalongkorn
revolutionize Siam.

crises, three Burmese armies converged on Ayutthaya and burned it to the ground, and with it the literature, writings, and dreams of the golden age.

One of the contested King's generals, Phraya Taksin, escaped the flaming city. He gathered the remnants of the Thai into an army, and in a bloody war, drove the Burmese back. Then he made himself King, and he built a capital—not at Ayutthaya, full of ghosts, but in the delta of the Chao Phraya, at the site of an old fortress called Thonburi, across the great river from where Bangkok now stands.

Taksin was a rough soldier, a man of the people, unconventional, earthy, erratic. Physically small, he was decisive and abrupt, and he could be grotesque. He once personally beheaded an officer who disobeyed him, and he ordered monks who disputed his power to haul dung, because he knew it degraded them.

Over the first years of his reign, he pulled the Kingdom back together, drove the Burmese back behind their borders, and even recovered some long-disputed territory in the north. When he had Burma under control, Taksin worked to recover the heritage lost in the flames of Ayutthaya, having scholars rewrite manuscripts and reconstruct inscriptions and art. He reestablished trade with China. (The Chinese merchant fleet, a crowd of enormous junks packed high with goods, made a yearly cycle of Southeast Asia, sailing west with the monsoon and going east again when the wind changed, bringing crockery, tea, paper, and made goods, and taking away Thai rice and sugar.)

The power of the monarchy went to Taksin's head. He began to see himself as the Buddha. Sycophants around him encouraged him in wilder delusions, that he had supernatural powers and could fly. He began to insist that even monks had to prostrate themselves before him. When they refused he humiliated them, and the monks turned against him. Finally some of his generals forced him to abdicate, and had him tried and executed.

THE CHAKKRI DYNASTY
The Rama-Kings of Thailand

After Taksin's tumultuous and gaudy career, Rama I was determined to restore the dignity of the monarchy. He moved the capital from Thonburi, which had become too small to suit the new King's purposes, across the river to its present site at Bangkok, then only a swampy flatland crisscrossed with elephant trails. Rama's overseers brought in thousands of *phrai* laborers to dig canals and build walls. At the core of the new city the first structure they built was a temple to house the most cherished relic of Rama's new dynasty: a little green image of Buddha he had brought from the Vientiane in Laos, before he became King, which was known as the Emerald Buddha.

Around this most sacred place grew up the Grand Palace, with its golden-roofed temples, its fantastic gardens, its splendid reception halls decorated with statuary and painting, its hundreds of dwelling places. The Palace was built within two years, a stunning feat of dedication, planning, and resources.

From the center of his splendid new city, Rama looked out and wanted still more magnificence. He invested every public move of the monarchy with a splendid accretion of ceremony. The King went about in a glow of gold and a ripple of peacock-feather fans, through splendidly painted halls and gardens alive with birds and orchids. His family also lived in opulence, surrounded by prostrated servants who attended them on their hands and knees.

Above all, Rama wanted to bring back in his new capital the now-legendary glory of Ayutthaya. Many of the buildings in the new site were copied from those of the devastated city, and Rama ordered the ruined buildings there torn down, and the bricks taken to the new site and raised up into new buildings, as if he could move the actual substance

The man who now became King was one of Taksin's oldest companions and most trusted generals. Born the fourth child of a Thai government official and his Chinese wife, he had risen to his place of power because of his ability and loyalty. He was not involved in the plot against Taksin; nonetheless, he acted decisively. Off fighting on the Cambodian border when Taksin was overthrown, he marched back to the capital, seized control with his army, put to death several of his rivals, and proclaimed himself King.

The name he chose for himself, Rama, was like a declaration of his intentions. Rama is the blue-skinned God-King who is the hero of the Ramayana, the great and multifarious epic that is told and retold throughout southern Asia. He is the perfect man, the ideal monarch. Taksin had only *thought* he was a god. Rama intended to act like one.

of the past. He ordered a canal dug straight through the center of the new city, in hopes that people would go out boating on it, and hold singing contests, as they had in Ayutthaya.

More and more the King was enveloping the monarchy in ceremony and ritual. Huge public displays attended every event of the life of the royal family. When one of the King's daughters was nearly drowned, the King declared a festival to celebrate her rescue. The tonsuring ceremonies for the royal princes, when their boy's locks were cut, could go on for days, a never-ending pageant of lavish banquets and performances with singing and dancing, food and money given away to everybody, and gaudy boat processions up and down the river.

But Thailand deserved to celebrate. Under Rama, the Kingdom was thriving. The Burmese invaded once more, and were driven back. The few foreigners who poked their noses in were adroitly managed. The Thais extracted from them whatever

SKETCHES FROM THE
STORYBOARDS:
*Anna's give and take
with the King becomes
more serious. Louis,
between them, bridges
the gap. Over his head,
the King and his mother
share a moment of
understanding.*

LOUIS REACHES OUT OVER THE RAILING —
IN B.G. ANNA GRABS FOR HIS BELT.

ANNA GRABS HER SON BY THE BELT AND
REIGNS HIM BACK IN.

good they could provide, while keeping the damages to a minimum. The splendor and wealth of Bangkok showed the whole world that Thailand was a great country.

Rama I died, and his son who followed him to the throne took the name of Rama II, proclaiming his intention of continuing his father's ways. But the vast court that surrounded the King, so necessary to his power and prestige, was also a breeding ground for conspiracy and intrigue. The plotting and treachery that beset Mongkut in *Anna and the King* were nothing new in the court of Siam.

Rama II had nothing of Mongkut's quality of tolerance. He was quick to take offense and to suppress even the slightest threat to his omnipotence. When a scandalous poem appeared that criticized him, Rama II set his eldest son, Chetsadabodin, to investigate. Chetsadabodin set about the task with zeal. Quickly he turned up the author of the poem, another half-brother of the King. In the course of Chetsadabodin's interrogation of this hapless man, he died. Nearly a dozen other people of the court were executed, too, for helping him. After that, no one dared speak a word against the King.

Rama II had other interests. He built a huge pleasure garden in Bangkok, with artificial lakes, pavilions, and rare plants and animals. In the middle of it, he wanted to raise a mountain, and so he caused rocks to be brought up from the sea and piled on the land.

This, people said, was what caused the great cholera epidemic of that year: the guardian spirits of the sea and the land had become angry at the mixing of their realms. The virulent epidemic was a new strain of the terrible disease, which struck the young and healthy, and could kill within hours. The monasteries could not burn the bodies of the dead fast enough, and corpses floated down the Chao Phraya. The King ordered special ceremonies, with the chanting of sacred texts and a procession of sacred objects around the city; to ward off the disaster, the royal gunners fired off cannon and beat drums. The King ordered the whole people to stop working, to let animals roam freely in the streets, to kill no living being—in short, to make merit, to do good to counterbalance the evil of the epidemic.

The epidemic tailed off. Few of the Thai associated it with what was probably its actual

KING MONGKUT : " I SIMPLY MEANT TO OPEN THE CONVERSATION IN CONTRAVERSIAL FASHION MEM IS SO FOND OF. "

ANNA : " I DO HAVE MY OWN OPINIONS ... BUT THEY ARE MERELY THAT. "

THE FOUR-ELEPHANT WAGON, WITH ANNA AND LOUIS; THE ROYAL ENTOURAGE, INCLUDING LADY THIANG AND TUPTIM, AND FA-YING AND THE CHILDREN.

Famed animal trainer Rona Brown worked with real elephants to pull this ornate cart. Brown and her crew recruited elephants from all over Malaysia to work in Anna and the King.

cause. Under Rama II, the outside world was discovering Thailand again. Besides the annual Chinese fleet, during the year just before the cholera epidemic several English and American ships had put into Bangkok to trade. The Thai government maintained a tight grip on them—some did good business; some did not. One of these merchant fleets brought the new cholera

into Thailand, like an omen of trouble to come.

In the 1820s the trouble seemed far away, like summer thunder. Burma attacked Thailand again, and the prince Chetsadabodin, who had shown such zeal in the pursuit of the libelous poem, led an army that repulsed the Burmese. Chetsadabodin was making himself very useful to his father—and this was causing a problem.

RIGHT: *At the Rice Festival, the Siamese celebrate the mainstay of their civilization: the unending bounty of the Chao Phraya rice fields.*

OPPOSITE PAGE: *The Rice Festival. Even today the King performs sacred ceremonies every year to ensure a good rice harvest.*

Chetsadabodin was Rama's eldest son, but his mother had been only a concubine. Rama's eldest son of princely rank was Mongkut, fifteen years younger. From the beginning, while relying on Chetsadabodin, the King had groomed young Mongkut to succeed him. But now the King's health was failing, and Mongkut was only eighteen.

In the winter of 1824, with the King clearly dying, Mongkut went into a monastery, as every male Thai did at the beginning of his adult life, to meditate, to study, and to gain merit for his parents. The Kingdom was uneasy. There were bad signs everywhere. Two white elephants had died—symbols of the sanctity of the Thai monarchy. And the King was clearly failing. In March, at last, Rama II passed on. The princes and ministers of the palace united to assure the succession. They passed over Mongkut in favor of his older, more experienced brother. Mongkut stayed a monk, and Chetsadabodin ascended the throne of the Thai.

Chetsadabodin took the name of Rama III. He was hardly upon the throne of Thailand when Burma erupted again, this time in a war with the British. The new King sided cautiously with the British, expecting a long struggle—and then watched in shock as the redcoats swept over southern Burma like a tide, forcing the King of Burma to his knees and seizing half his Kingdom in a space of weeks.

The Thais were stunned. Burma had always been a power in Southeast Asia. The Thai had cooperated with the British before, and even allowed some British trade, but now their suspicions were engaged. When a British envoy came, hoping to negotiate a trading treaty, the King put him off and made preparations to defend the Kingdom against attack, bringing out the *phrai* to dig huge canals and raise fortresses in the delta of the Chao Phraya. To support this, Rama III raised more taxes, and he instituted a state lottery.

Yet the British were seeping into his country.

The Drama of the Sun and Moon. Jenny Beavan's sumptuous costumes adorn this lavish folk tale, half play and half dance.

They came first as traders, of course, seemingly harmless; they even had some good ideas, which the Thai appropriated as they cared to, learning to build steamships and square-rigged sailing ships in the great boat basins of Bangkok. But the clash of values was inevitable. Each flare of tempers was a fundamental difference of perspective.

In 1831, three British traders went out one morning along the river to shoot birds; one wandered onto the grounds of a monastery and killed two pigeons. The monks set on him, outraged. The indignant traders went to the King and threatened to bring in warships and fire on the royal palace if he did not punish the monks severely.

Rama, of course, did nothing to the monks, but the event proved forcefully how different the two cultures were from each other. And the British seemed unstoppable. When British armies defeated China, in the Opium Wars in 1839 and 1841, the whole Thai universe shook. China, the Central Country, was in Thai eyes the greatest power on earth, while Britain was only a little island somewhere off in the cold mists of the north. Yet here was the Emperor of China, humbled before a red-coat officer.

Rama III now saw every Westerner—and every Western idea—as a threat and an enemy. He worked to close down Thailand against the West, ejecting the prominent merchants, and trying to uproot the missionaries established in Bangkok.

Then, in 1849, cholera struck the Kingdom. Thousands died. The King did as tradition bade him, a tactic designed to meet the bad influence of the sickness by creating good influences throughout the Kingdom: no one had to work, there were processions and public prayers, and captive animals were set free. When the Christian missionaries refused to go along with this, seeing it as paganism, the King

was sure that they intended to see all Thailand die.

Faced with his rage, the Christians hastily decided to declare the ceremonies to be civil ones, not religious, and hence not pagan, but the King had many of them arrested, and he turned even more hostile to Western overtures to open trade.

But even now, rumors persisted in the British circles of Singapore that there were two princes at the Siamese court who liked foreign ideas and were still willing to receive people from the West. These two princes were Mongkut and his younger brother, Itsaret, both of whom were candidates for the throne of Thailand when Rama III died—and in 1850, Rama III fell unexpectedly and mortally ill.

DECORATION TO BE

EARLY THAILAND:
A Chinese Traveler Reports Back Home

ABOVE AND NEXT PAGE: *The magnificent banquet scene has appeared in every version of Anna's story—but never as splendidly as this.*

In 1433, a fleet of Chinese junks sailed into the Chao Phraya, bringing presents and taking notes; one of the Chinese sent back this report to the Imperial Government:

The country is a thousand li in circumference, the outer mountains being steep and rugged, and the inner land wet and swampy . . . the climate varies—sometimes cold, sometimes hot.

The house in which the king resides is rather elegant, neat, and clean. The houses of the populace are constructed in storeyed form; [in the upper part] of the house they do not join planks together [to make a floor], but they use the wood of the areca-palm, which they cleave into strips resembling bamboo splits; [these strips] are laid close together and bound very securely with rattans; on [this plat-form] they spread rattan mats and bamboo matting, and on these they do all their sitting, sleeping, eating, and resting.

As to the king's dress he uses a white cloth to wind around his head; on the upper [part of his body] he wears no garment; [and] round the lower [part he wears] a silk-embroidered kerchief, adding a waist-band of brocaded silk-gauze. When going about he mounts an elephant or else rides in a sedan-chair, while a man holds [over him] a gold-handled umbrella made of chiao-chang leaves, [which is] very elegant. The king is a man of the So-Li race, and a firm believer in the Buddhist religion.

In this country the people who become priests or become nuns are exceedingly numerous; the habit of the priests and nuns is somewhat the same as in the Central Country [China]; and they too live in nunneries and monasteries, fasting and doing penance.

—from "The Overall Survey of the Ocean's Shores"

MONGKUT
A King with a Common Touch

His Majesty received me and my little boy most kindly. After an interval of silence he clapped his hands lightly and instantly the lower hall was filled with female slaves. A word or two dropped from his lips, bowed every head and dispersed the attendants. But they presently returned laden, some with boxes containing books, slates, pens, pencils, and ink; others with lighted tapers and vases filled with the white lotos, which they set down before the gilded chairs.

At a signal from the King, the priests chanted a hymn from the "P'ra-jana Para-mita" [Transcendental Wisdom]; and then a burst of music announced the entrance of the princes and the princesses, my future pupils. They advanced in the order of their ages. The Princess Ying You Wahlacks ("First-born among Women"), having precedence, approached and prostrated herself before her royal father, the others following her example. I admired the beauty of her skin, the delicacy of her form, and the subdued luster of her dreamy eyes. The King took her gently by the hand, and presented me to her, saying simply, "The English teacher." Her greeting was quiet and self-possessed. Taking both my hands, she bowed, and touched them with her forehead; then, at a word from the king, retired to her place on the right. One by one, in like manner, all the royal children were presented and saluted me; and the music ceased.*

—from *The English Governess*

Mongkut, who was the eldest son of King Rama II and his Queen, had grown up in his father's court, studying to become King himself, passing every day in elaborate rituals, and waited on hand and foot by an army of slaves. Early on, his father advanced him with huge public ceremonies at his

King Mongkut planned the Anniversary Banquet in an effort to show English nobles and diplomats how civilized a ruler he could be.

various rites of passage. At the age of eighteen, as tradition required, he entered the monastery; then suddenly his father died. His elder brother became Rama III. Mongkut remained in the yellow robe.

He spent the early years of his monkhood in Wat Samorai, a monastery on the edge of Bangkok. There he did more than meditate and study ancient texts. Mongkut was a brilliant man. He educated himself, and, like all autodidacts, he was both utterly confident of his own opinions and profoundly open-minded: his skepticism shocked Anna Leonowens as much as the breadth of his understanding impressed her.

While he was in Wat Samorai he became friends with a French missionary, with whom he argued the relative merits of Buddhism and Christianity. From this Frenchman he learned French and a little Latin, and got books on scientific matters. In between his meditations and his study of sacred texts, Mongkut read Voltaire, and learned astronomy; he could predict eclipses, which startled and impressed all the Thai, who considered eclipses to happen when a sky-dwelling dragon devoured the moon.

Mongkut was vigorous and ambitious, even in the monastery, where he rose to prominence. At some point he talked with a Burmese monk who was part of a movement among the Burmese *sangha* to purify the ritual, and Mongkut came to believe that the ritual in Thailand had become corrupted also. He began to perform a purified ordination, which made him very controversial in the *sangha*, raising an opposition he simply ignored.

He was convinced that superstitions and corruptions had infiltrated Thai religious practice and he worked steadily to eradicate them. Possibly his conversations with the French priest had given him a new perspective on the historical development of religion. Certainly, however, he was open to new ideas from unexpected sources, since Burma was still Thailand's arch-rival and old-est enemy. He also brought in a printing press, on which he printed books and pamphlets in both Thai and English.

Mongkut's freedom of mind did not amuse his superiors. In 1836, his brother Rama III had him appointed abbot of a new monastery in the heart of Bangkok, where the King could keep an eye on him.

Itsaret, Mongkut's younger brother, was also very open to (even fascinated by) Western ideas. He was also beloved of the people, who were chafing under Rama's heavy taxes. Itsaret lacked Mongkut's deepness of purpose and power of mind; to him, Western ideas were fun, like the little steamboat in which he puttered up and down the Chao Phraya while admiring crowds lined the riverbank to cheer.

But the steamboats were very serious business, part of the allure of the West that even the King could not ignore, the ideas and technology that accompanied the guns and the goods and the

Anna plunges into the marketplace, into all the tastes and smells and colors and zest of Siam.

OPPOSITE PAGE: *Jodie Foster is beautiful as Anna, developing her vulnerability as well as her resolution and quick wit, to give us a full-bodied portrait of a remarkable woman.*

71

money. The more the King tried to suppress Western ideas, the more threatening they became.

But Thai society was strong, its economy solidly built on the great rice fields of the Chao Phraya Valley, on the enormous teak forests, the tin mines, the hardheaded diligence of the people, and a long-standing system of trade. The Buddhist ethical system, with its emphasis on compassion, self-denial, and calm, knit the country together into a single fabric of ritual and belief; the people themselves were capable, innovative, able to use new ideas without succumbing to their pernicious elements. Of all the countries in Southeast Asia, Thailand was best prepared to stay free.

It all depended on the King—on who became King, now that Rama III was dying. Once again, the succession turned on the decisions of the close circle of ministers and princes who surrounded the dying monarch. Once again, this council proved its farsightedness. Passing over Rama III's own sons, who were rowdy, indolent, and mindless, they gave the throne to Mongkut. They associated Itsaret with his older brother, possibly to mollify the younger man's ambitions, but after twenty-seven years in the monastery, Mongkut now became King of Siam.

The most unconventional of all Thailand's Kings began his reign in a most conventional way, adopting the reign-name Rama IV, and lavishing a fortune on his anointing festivities, including a boat procession during which boatmen dropped overboard hundreds of gaily painted wooden boxes shaped like fruit and filled with money, gifts to the hordes of people thronging the shore.

But Mongkut was a different kind of King. He understood where the real power was; on the face of it, he was absolute monarch of Siam, but in practice, the council of his advisers managed the Kingdom's affairs. Among these were two men especially who had served for decades and whose wise counsel was vital to the King. At special ceremonies awarding them new titles, it is said that the King

The royal wives share sweets and gossip—the main subject, their mutual husband and the Englishwoman!

prostrated himself before these two men, an unprecedented act of humility.

Mongkut also allowed people to gaze upon the King's face, which had always been forbidden. From the beginning he went often and openly among his people, with processions and ceremonies but also in spontaneous ways; when his first steamboat was launched, he amazed everybody by coming on board and insisting on a ride up and down the Chao Phraya.

Immediately after he became King, Mongkut began the delicate process of opening his realm to the West. Everyone in Southeast Asia now expected the British would seize Siam. Fortunately for the first two years of Mongkut's reign the British were occupied with absorbing another piece of Burma. Mongkut made use of the time. Rama III had left him a full treasury, and the King began an ambitious series of canals and forts, including a fort built especially to greet foreign ships as they approached Bangkok—and to protect the Chao Phraya from an invading navy.

These coast defenses were vital to the Thai. Britain's war with Burma was going in the now-familiar way: Britain redcoats pounded the Burmese army, and in 1853 the King of Burma sued for peace. That left the British free to deal with the Thai.

In 1855, John Bowring, Governor of the British Crown Colony of Hong Kong, came to Bangkok to negotiate another trade treaty. Previous treaty negotiations had come up empty, and for a while it seemed that this session would fail also; Mongkut was a hard bargainer who let his ministers do the front work and strung Bowring along to get the best terms possible. The Governor of Hong Kong was himself a steady and patient haggler, but there was a rising grumble among the British behind him that perhaps they ought to stop haggling with these arrogant and ignorant Thai, that they should go in and take over, for the good of all. Then, in 1856, while the King still had Bowring dangling, an envoy arrived from American President Franklin Pierce.

This was the opening that the King had needed. He made a quick treaty with the Americans, and then with half a dozen other powers, including the Prussians and the Hanseatic League, and by the time Bowring got the British treaty the Empire was only one country among many struggling for the trade of rich Bangkok. Siam might get chewed on, but now it was unlikely to be swallowed whole.

But the treaties were only the beginning. Opening Siam meant letting in the sweeping changes of modernity. Suddenly there was a stream of foreigners into the Kingdom, not missionaries, but traders. They needed houses, churches, warehouses, stores, and a waterfront—and built them. They needed currency with which to do their trading. For a while the Thai mint couldn't keep up with the demand for new silver baht; finally they changed the design to one that was easier to make. (Pre-Mongkut baht were bullet-shaped, reflecting the early use of cowry shells for money.)

The Thai fascination with foreign technology continued, as the King himself enthusiastically ordered more steamboats, and imported steam engines for a rice mill and timber mills. Soon banks of foreign warehouses ranged along the shores of the river, and wooden wharves ran out like fingers into the green water. The whole harbor was now always full of ships, British East Indiamen beside the usual junks, and American clipper ships, and French and Dutch vessels also, among the scurry of the lighters, and the swift dart of Thai riverboats going up and down. In the floating markets, the babble of English and French and a dozen other exotic languages competed with Thai, and goods from all over the world went up for sale, a wild clutter of imported manufactures among the usual stalls of flowers and fruit and cloth. Above all this bustle, above the new rooftops of the warehouses and the Western-style houses going up behind the water-

front, the golden pagodas of the great temples overlooked a world that, though much the same for centuries, was now changing every day.

There were profound changes underway in Thai society, too. Educated and ambitious young men now were inclined to go into business and not the monasteries. Some of these young men began to adopt other Western ideas, like growing their hair out, sporting mustaches, looking with scorn on the practice of chewing betel-nuts, and wearing shoes and socks. Conservative Thais blamed the King for the uncertainties of change, and predicted the imminent and terrible collapse of the country. Some younger people said Siam wasn't changing fast enough.

Yet Mongkut seemed fearless in his course. As much as he loved the new Western ideas with their myriad practical applications, he had great confidence in his own people and their traditions. He himself loved the challenge of intellectual combat, and was always willing to argue his own point of view—as Anna herself found out at once.

Mongkut's instinct was to prove people wrong, not to suppress them. He never tried to muzzle even the most annoying (if most harmless) of his opponents, the American missionary Dr. Dan Beach Bradley, who arrived in Bangkok in the 1830s.

Bradley brought many wonderful innovations with him: he had arrived with a printing press, the first in Thailand; he administered the first vaccinations of the Thai and performed the first surgery. The King supported his medical work and tolerated his efforts to convert the Thai, efforts that were utterly unsuccessful. Dr. Bradley, shocked at the general unwillingness of the Thai to change their faith of centuries, fulminated against the King in his *Bangkok Recorder*.

Mongkut could have shut him down but did not. Instead, he got his own printing press and published his own retorts to Bradley and had them distributed all over the capital—especially in the foreign quarter.

The only time Mongkut put his foot down with regard to the zealous Bradleys was when he invited Bradley's wife and another missionary woman, Mrs. Mattoon, to come into the harem and teach his wives English. When they tried to teach Christianity also, he sent them packing, and never let them inside the palace again. Nonetheless, he used these people when they were convenient to him: he got Bradley to write letters to the English papers in the colonies with approving descriptions of Mongkut and his policies.

Mongkut was right. His country was strong enough to survive the tidal wave of the Western assault. The French took Vietnam and Laos and eyed Cambodia, the British took Burma, and the Dutch held Indonesia. All these ancient cultures were put through the grinder of abrupt, often violent change; only the Thai remained in control of their own destiny. A good deal of the credit goes to King Mongkut.

PREVIOUS PAGE:
At the summer palace, on the shore of the Andaman Sea, Anna's pupils release a fleet of fragile tiny luminaries upon the water.

The King, meditative. Mongkut was a brilliant man, who studied several languages and delighted in Western science and technology—and cigars.

OPPOSITE PAGE:
Mongkut reads a letter from President Abraham Lincoln.

The King at work in his office, surrounded by books and gadgets.

Tuptim's fatal love letter.

Besides bringing in the ideas they needed to keep pace with the West, he worked hard to present a suitably royal and respected image to the world. Yet he had a common touch, perhaps learned during his long years in the monkhood, when every day he had gone out to beg for his supper. Far more than any Thai King before or since, he made many public appearances, involving himself often in the lives of ordinary folk, giving away food and money to the poor and elderly, and observing cases in his courts to make sure the settlements were fair. He kept up a famous correspondence with foreign heads of state, from Queen Victoria and Napoleon III to Abraham Lincoln. He sent for an English schoolteacher from Singapore to educate his children and his wives.

A familiar problem shadowed his reign. In 1866, the King's brother Itsaret died, leaving the Crown with no obvious and designated successor. Mongkut's eldest son of princely rank, Anna Leonowens's student Prince Chulalongkorn, was only eleven, although already he showed the brilliance and steadiness necessary to become King.

Anna wrote of him,

He was attentive to his studies, serene, and gentle, invariably affectionate to his old aunt and his younger brothers, and for the poor ever sympathetic, with a warm, generous heart. He pursued his studies assiduously, and seemed to overcome the difficulties and obstacles he encountered in the course of them with a resolution that gained strength as his mind gained ideas. As often as he effectually accomplished something, he indulged in ecstasies of rejoicing over the new thought, that was an inspiring discovery to him of his actual poverty of knowledge, his possibilities of intellectual opulence.

Now, a little late, Mongkut turned to this boy for his successor. The young prince was brought more and more forward into the public eye. His topknot cutting ceremonies lasted for seven days

and were marvels of elaboration. The topknot cutting ceremony was of ancient Brahminic lineage and marked the passage of the youth into manhood. For Mongkut, already in his sixties, the issue of a successor was pressing.

The King, however, was living his life to the hilt. He had a quick, violent temper, but he was also very engaging when he wanted to be. His court was always a whirl of activity, and the King was always at its center. Every year on his birthday, he had a splendid banquet, to which he invited all the eminent foreigners in Bangkok: the British, French, and all the other consuls, the rich merchants, and the missionary doctors—to them he showed off his skillful use of Western tableware as well as his wit and charm.

As a self-taught man, Mongkut loved to dazzle people around him with bits of knowledge. In conversation with Westerners he would often slip in little comments on the language. Once, completely out of the blue, he told Bowring, the Governor of Hong Kong who negotiated the groundbreaking treaty, "You have two terms, one the vulgar, leap-year—the other, the classical—bissextile." There

was no point to the remark, except to demonstrate the King's erudition, a subject which endlessly delighted Mongkut.

He himself proved to the world that East and West could meet, and very happily. He reveled in such Western toys as steam engines and printing presses, yet he remained a devout Buddhist. His faith underlay his calm in the face of chaotic change. He went all around the country, on tours of monasteries, accepting gifts of white elephants, building temples and palaces; his people loved him because they knew him, they saw him among them, and they took heart from his courage.

He was a devotee of the Copernican solar system, which went counter to the traditional Thai model, and in 1868 he organized an expedition of his court, with ten French scientists and a swarm of nobles and princes, to watch an eclipse that would occur, he predicted, over the southern part of the country. The eclipse happened just as he had foretold. As he had not foretold, he and many of his court, including his young son Prince Chulalongkorn, caught malaria in the southern swamps.

The prince recovered, but the King died. Thailand had lost the most extraordinary of all its extraordinary Kings.

Largely because of Mongkut's work, the Thai escaped being colonized. They were hurled headlong into the rapid modernization that would wrack the whole world over the next few decades but they took with them the tools to establish a new society. Mongkut's greatest achievements would not be realized until his son's reign, and then in ways that would have taken the old King quite aback: the abolition of slavery and prostration, the overhaul of the government into a modern state. But all of this grew from the seeds that Mongkut planted. His openness to ideas from the West, his confidence in his own culture's ability to absorb new ideas and keep its integrity, and his willingness to experiment and change formed the basis for his great son's work.

Above all, he was not afraid of the future, but relished its challenge.

Mongkut himself bridged the gulf between the two cultures. Even his idiosyncratic English was symbolic of his ability to enter into the new world while remaining Thai to the core. Here again, Anna Leonowens gives us invaluable insight. She shows the world the human side of the King, his tenderness with his children, his sense of humor, his charisma. It's only fitting that their story should be told again in *Anna and the King*, in a setting as splendid as the Grand Palace of this most endearingly human King, with his great heart and quick wit and thoroughgoing zest for life.

THE EXCHANGE OF LETTERS
Between Mongkut and Abraham Lincoln

Somdetch Phra Paramendr Maha Mongkut, by the blessing of the highest superagency of the whole universe, the King of Siam, the sovereign of all interior tributary countries adjacent and around in every direction, viz., Laws of Shiengs on northwestern and northern, Law Kaus on northern to northeastern to southeastern, most of the Malay Peninsula on southern and southwestern, and Kariengs on the western and northwestern points, and the professor of the Magadhe language and Budhistical literature, &c., &c., &c., to his most respected excellent presidency, the President of the United States of America, who having been chosen by the citizens of the United States as most distinguished, was made president and chief magistrate in the affairs of the nation for an appointed time of office.

It has occurred to us that if on the continent of America there should be several pairs of young male elephants turned loose in forest where there was an abundance of water and grass, in any

region under the sun's declination, both north and south, called by the English the torrid zone, and all were forbidden to molest them, to attempt to raise them would be well. And if the climate there should prove favorable to elephants we are of an opinion that after a while they will increase until they become large herds, as there are here on the continent of Asia, until the inhabitants of America will be able to catch and tame and use them as beasts of burthen, making them of benefit to the country, since elephants, being animals of great size and strength, can bear burdens and travel through dense woods and matted jungle where no carriage and cartroads have yet been made.

We on our part will procure young male and female elephants, and forward them, one or two pairs at a time.

When the elephants are on the board the ship, let a steamer take it in tow, that it may reach America as rapidly as possible, before they become wasted and diseased by the voyage.

When they arrive in America, do not let them be taken to a cold climate, out of the regions under the sun's declinations, or torrid zone, but let them with all haste be turned out to run wild in some jungle suitable for them, not confining them any length of time.

If these means can be done, we trust that elephants will propagate their species hereafter in the continent of America.

The President responded with proper gravity and dignity.

I appreciate most highly your Majesty's tender of good offices in forwarding to this government a stock from which a supply of elephants might be raised on our own soil. This government would not hesitate to avail itself of so generous an offer if the object were one which could be made practically useful in the present condition of the United States. Our political jurisdiction, however, does not reach a latitude so low as to favor the multiplication of the

elephant. And steam on land, as well as on water, has been our best and most efficient agent of transportation and internal commerce.

I shall have occasion at no distant day to transmit your Majesty some token or indication of the high sense which this government entertains of your Majesty's friendship.

Meantime, wishing for your Majesty a long and happy life, and for the generous and emulous people of Siam, the highest prosperity. I commend both to the blessings of Almighty God.

> Your good friend,
> Abraham Lincoln
> Washington, February 3, 1862
> By the President,
> William H. Seward, Secretary of State

ANNA AFTER SIAM
A Woman of the World

Even after she left Siam, Anna Leonowens remained one of the most fascinating and original women of her time. After Bangkok she stayed in Great Britain just long enough to park Louis in school and pick up Avis, now a pretty, shy girl of fourteen, before moving to the United States. Perhaps in her heart she knew already her Thai

adventure was over. In New York, she heard the news of Mongkut's death, and Chulalongkorn's election as King, under a Regency of men she knew were not friendly to the West. She would not be going back to Siam.

There was work to be done in America. She and Avis started a school, in New Brighton on Staten Island, in New York City, and Anna began to write. In 1870, her first four stories appeared in the *Atlantic Monthly*, the foremost magazine of its day, and Anna Leonowens became a sensation.

She had a gift for description; she made people feel that they were standing in the golden glow of a Thai sunset, looking out over the burnished river toward the great sky-piercing spires of the wats. She played, too, on the themes so close to her heart; she filled her stories with the terrors of slavery and the grim lives of the captive women in the harem. Her audiences were insatiable.

Soon she was giving lectures to packed halls of people sitting rapt on her every word as, without any notes or cues, she bubbled up a steady fountain of stories and descriptions of the fabled Oriental Kingdom. She became an overnight success. She met most of the great authors of her time—including, to her delight, Harriett Beecher Stowe, whose *Uncle Tom's Cabin* had so captivated Lady Son Klin, half a world away.

OPPOSITE PAGE AND ABOVE: *After them come the King's elephants, each carrying a field piece. Elephants are still widely employed in Malaysia for heavy labor; but animal trainer Rona Brown taught them to do things their masters never dreamt of.*

OPPOSITE PAGE:
Monks file out of the
Temple of the Emerald
Buddha after Prince
Chulalongkorn's
Ceremony of Noviciation,
when he discards the
trappings of opulent
royalty for the plain
white robe of a novice
monk. Every future King
must perform this ritual.

In 1878, Avis married a handsome and successful banker, Thomas Fyshe, whose business was in Halifax, Nova Scotia, in Canada. Avis and her new husband set up their household in Halifax, and Anna moved in with them. Not that Anna was always there to baby-sit or give advice. Her lectures took her around the country, and in 1880, the popular magazine *Youth's Companion* sent her as a correspondent to tour Russia—by herself.

Anna took up this challenge as eagerly as she had gone to Siam. She went all around the Tsar's huge empire, from the wooden cities with their gaudy onion-domed cathedrals to the huts of peasants in the great wheat fields, meeting noblemen, farmers, and students alike and sending back dispatches to the magazine.

These articles, too, were a huge success. Whether it was in the description of a nobleman's dinner, or the baptism of a peasant baby, or the plight of young women students at the Russian universities—Anna brought it all vividly to life. The *Youth's Companion* offered her full-time job as an editor, but she turned it down to stay with her family—Avis's steadily growing brood, in whose education she took a central role.

She still had her favorite causes. In Halifax, she campaigned for a better jail and better treatment of the inmates as well as against the abuse of children, and she founded the Halifax School of Art & Design. But surely her finest hour, after Siam, was an impromptu speech for women's suffrage in the provincial assembly.

Male Canada was stiffly resisting the idea of allowing women to take their turn at the ballot box. The old Victorian notions of woman's place were alive and well in the minds of men. One legislator announced that letting women vote would interfere with the true vocation of the female sex, which was "first the bearing and bringing up of children, and this is the highest. Second, the creating of home and the beautifying of life . . . Third, to charm men and make the world pleasant, sweet and agreeable to live in. Fourth, to be kindly and loving, to be sweet and to be cherished, to be weak and confiding, to be protected and to be the object of man's devotion."

This infuriated Anna. In the gallery above the legislature, she stood up and threw Queen Victoria herself in his face. A true woman, she declared, was not the "servant and plaything of a man," but "a true helpmeet and co-worker." To prove it, she then and there invited all the women in Canada to stop paying their taxes until they got the vote.

The roar of approval shook the legislature. Anna herself was living proof of the falsehood of the Victorian caricature and the value of her threat. On her own, unprotected and decidedly not weak, she was making a handsome income on her writing and lecturing; she was regularly paid $60 a night to talk, at a time when a workingman made $40 a month, or less. Anyone who thought a woman needed a man had not met Anna Leonowens.

By this time, she knew, also, that the seeds she had planted in Siam had taken root. In 1884, the Thai Foreign Minister came to New York, and Anna went for a private audience—since he was none other than Prince Krita, one of her favorite pupils. He told her that Chulalongkorn, now King, was intent on abolishing slavery and prostration. And in 1897, Chulalongkorn himself received her, when that energetic and far-traveling King visited London. Her work in Siam had succeeded far beyond what she could have hoped for. Her pupils were remaking the Kingdom of the Free into a modern state.

Anna's children grew up to reflect on their widely different childhoods. Daughter Avis, raised in an English boarding school, went on to become the true Victorian angel of the house. She bore her husband Thomas Fyshe eight children, and made a sumptuous home for her husband, her children, and her mother. She was quiet, letting Anna and

mother becoming increasingly unhappy with his profligate and aimless ways. Then, abruptly, he took himself off to Thailand.

There he fell in again with his childhood chums, Chulalongkorn and his brothers. Their friendship quickly revived. Louis went into the Thai army and married one of Chulalongkorn's sisters. His favorite occupation, though, was roaming through the mountains and forests of wild Thailand, finding new birds and plants, and reveling in the magnificence of nature. He made himself a fortune cutting teak from the upland jungles. There were rumors that in the backcountry he lived like a great Thai noble, with his own harem and court. When his wife the Princess died, he came out of the jungle to take his two small children away to their grandmother in Canada to let Anna and Avis raise them, but then he returned to Thailand, where he was happiest. Anna had been right: Louis Leonowens was a Thai at heart.

The family connection to Thailand was strong. One of Anna's grandsons, James Fyshe, went to Thailand to serve as chief medical officer.

After Avis's death Anna lost much of her old verve. She lived a quieter life, and died on January 19, 1915. Her funeral procession wound down the street and up the hill behind and it seemed all of Canada had come out to mourn her. And surely all those people knew she was a remarkable woman.

But no one knew how remarkable. Anna had hidden the truth about her past away. All these people coming to see her buried believed she was the daughter of an English officer, a genteel upper-class Englishwoman who through unforeseeable circumstances somehow found herself in Bangkok teaching Siamese children to speak English. But the truth is astonishing.

She was born and educated in a soldier's barracks. She was nearly shunted away into the brutal drudgery of a soldier's wife. Instead, she launched

Thomas dominate the brilliant conversations around the dinner table; but when she suddenly died of food poisoning, early in the new century, both her mother and her husband lost the main prop of their daily lives.

Louis, on the other hand, had grown up in a harem. He loved to ride and talk and ramble around the countryside, and his infectious charm ingratiated him with everybody—except his teachers at the Irish boarding school his mother had hoped would "civilize" him. He left school as soon as he could, and came to America to his mother and sister. There, he rattled around awhile, taking odd jobs and roaming around the country, his

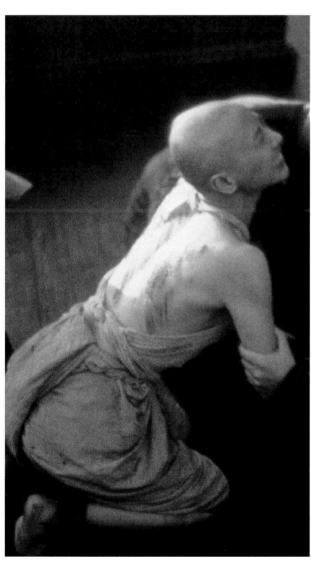

herself on the adventure of a lifetime, learning, teaching others, and always pursuing her high ideals of justice and equality. With her wits and her skill with the pen, she rose to become one of the preeminent women of her time. Truly, Anna Leonowens was a match for a king.

BUDDHISM:
Not the Theory But the Practice

It's only fitting that Buddhism figures so prominently in *Anna and the King*. Whether it's Mongkut praying before the Emerald Buddha, or a procession of monks in their yellow robes, scene after scene reminds us of the spiritual basis for Thai society.

At the heart of all Buddhism lies the belief that the world of phenomena, the outward and visible universe, is an illusion, and that all suffering and evil arise from adherence to this illusion. Theravada Buddhism, the older of the two great strands of this faith, holds that, through diligent practice of the Eightfold Way, individual people can see through the illusion, experience reality directly, and pass

97

into nirvana, the state of enlightenment that is oneness with Buddha and the universe.

Along the way to nirvana, Buddhists can acquire merit through good deeds and thoughtfulness to others. The Eightfold Way, which Buddha preached, is a program of right thinking, right actions, and meditation that has come to appeal to millions of people around the world for its orderliness, its calm, and its emphasis on compassion and service to others.

All of Thai life is steeped in Buddhism. The pagodas of the great wats still rule the skyline of Bangkok, and in each backcountry village there is another wat, blending the local, daily rituals of country life into the tremendous liturgy of the cosmos. The abbot is often the most powerful man in the village, settling disputes and making decisions for the whole community.

Even now, every Thai man is expected to spend some part of his life in a monastery, praying, study-

ing, and making merit for his parents. His head and eyebrows shaved, he dons the saffron-colored robe and goes into a timeless world that was old before the Thai left China, in which he has nothing, owns nothing, depends on the goodwill of others for every morsel of food in his mouth. He meditates, attempting to quiet his mind until he achieves the perfect stillness and peace of thoughtlessness, when in a leap of recognition he may see the great truth that is all around us all the time. He recites ancient texts. He cares for the helpless; many a monastery in Thailand takes in unwanted animals and keeps them until they die. All this stores up a steady supply of goodness that warms the whole Kingdom. Everywhere, monks are revered; they even get the best seats on the bus.

The fundamental beauty of Thai life owes as much to Buddhism as it does to the extraordinary loveliness of their landscape. Buddhism supplies a sense of balance, of wholeness, that supports the people through the shocks and quakes of modern

Tuptim, crushed but not broken.

OPPOSITE PAGE:
Tuptim endures her suffering with the strength of the innocent.

Guards drag the tortured Balat into the Hall of Justice to testify.

life. Seeking merit, the Thai make offerings of flowers, set free flocks of birds, help the poor and the weak and the suffering. The calm and courtesy so striking among the Thai derive from the belief that anger, egotism, pride, and selfishness all spring from the illusion of things and from the grasping and greed that clings to the illusion.

Through diligent practice, the Buddhist struggles to free himself from the illusion of his own existence, a misconception that binds him to the endless cycle of life, death, and rebirth. By acquiring merit, a Buddhist hopes to guarantee that he will be reborn into a better life; wickedness and greed earn him a rebirth as something much lower, such as an animal, or an insect. The ultimate goal is to escape from the wheel of life entirely, to pass into *nirvana*, and merge with the glowing reality that is the only truth: the oneness and "now-ness" of all.

Still, it is not belief that leads the Buddhist higher, but practice; not the goal, but the Path. The emphasis is always on works, on service to others,

self-sacrifice for the sake of others, self-discipline, and a profound self-awareness that is the opposite of selfishness. Small wonder that even Christian missionaries came grudgingly to admire Buddhism. A member of the French academy, M. Laboulaye, said, "It is difficult to comprehend how men, not aided by revelation, could have soared so high and approached so near the truth."

CHULALONGKORN:
Anna's Star Pupil
Comes to Power

He often deplored with me the cruelty with which the slaves were treated, and, young as he was, did much to inculcate kindness toward them among his immediate attendants. He was a conscientious lad, of pensive habit and gentle temper. . . . Speaking of slavery one day, he said to me: "These are not slaves, but nobles; they know how to bear. It is we,

Sketches from the director's book help shape the scene even before it exists. Here, a few lines convey the elegance and grandeur of Siamese public life, as well as its rigorous order. The sketch conveys as well the dark threat spreading over Mongkut and his family and kingdom.

the princes, who have yet to learn which is the more noble, the oppressor or the oppressed.

—from *The English Governess*

When King Mongkut died, his son Prince Chulalongkorn, who would become Rama IV, was only fifteen. He had not been the King's heir until very late in Mongkut's reign, but as Mongkut lay dying the old King arranged carefully for his son's succession.

As Regent for the boy King, he named the Kingdom's chief minister, a member of the powerful Bunnak family whose own father had guaranteed the throne for Mongkut, seventeen years before.

The Thai system of bureaucracy, in which the most powerful ministries had their own sources of revenue, tended to concentrate administrative power in the hands of a few great families. By the time of Chulalongkorn's succession, although the Thais considered their King to be absolute, the real power in the monarchy lay with the huge family of the Regent, which held positions throughout the government. The Regent himself, Sisuriyawong, through his various offices, commanded the Thai army, controlled the economy, and administered foreign affairs. When asked, later, why he had not deposed the boy King and assumed the throne himself, he said, "Because I already had everything I wanted."

106

The Regent utterly dominated the first five years of Chulalongkorn's reign. The boy King said later that he felt totally alone and lonely, with no one to confide in or to support him. He was quickly folded into the decorative life of the court, attending public rituals, performing the King's ceremonial duties, and receiving in public, to a twenty-one-gun salute, a letter from Queen Victoria.

At seventeen, he went on tour to Singapore and the Dutch Indonesian colony of Batavia, to observe for himself how Westerners administrated their governments; he visited post offices and jails, schools and hospitals and factories, seeing everything first-hand. In Singapore he encountered an American circus, which he invited back with him to Bangkok, to perform in the palace.

That done, he wanted to go to Europe, but the Regent vetoed the idea and sent him instead to India for three months. Even without the exotic tastes of Europe, all this foreign travel filled the young King with ideas; when he came home from India, he refused to allow anyone to prostrate himself in the royal presence, a practice he now considered degrading both to the person doing the prostrating and the person for whom it was done.

He told Anna that:

The steamboat that will take the King's children away to safety. Mongkut was enthusiastic about steam energy and had several steamboats built while he was King.

If he ever lived to reign over Siam, he would reign over a free and not an enslaved nation; that it would be his pride and joy to restore to his Kingdom the original constitution under which it was first planted by a small colony of hardy and brave Buddhists, who had fled their native country, Magadah, to escape the religious persecution of the brahminical priests, who had arrived at Ayutthya and there established themselves under one of their leaders, who was at once priest and king. They called the spot they occupied Muang Thai—*the kingdom of the free. . . .*

He itched to govern his country. Restrained from actually doing anything meaningful, he drilled his large bodyguard in European military discipline, as well as having them learn administration and literature. The boy who felt so alone was surrounding himself with people who thought as he did.

Siam was in upheaval, a slow-motion revolution. The Kingdom was not going through the wringer of colonization, but its traditional way of life was under tremendous pressure nonetheless.

Values taken for granted for centuries were coming under a blast of scrutiny. Although Bangkok took the first brunt of the waves of foreign impact, the backcountry was only now opening up; there was talk of a railroad, of a telegraph, of a post office, for which all houses had to be numbered. Already some young Thai aristocrats were going to England for their educations, and coming back with radicalized values about class and money and power.

In 1873 Chulalongkorn became of major age and was anointed King. He began at once to modernize his government. His first proclamation did away with prostration. He replaced the traditional tax structure with a less exploitive system. He proposed to abolish slavery over a period of a generation; he began to root out corruption, to reorganize the government from top to bottom. In order to ram through his reforms and circumvent the power of the great families in their entrenched ministries, he founded new institutions packed with his followers.

The society, already quaking with the abruptness of change, was not ready for so much reform.

The Second King was Wichaichan, the son of Mongkut's brother Itsaret, and a rival of Chulalongkorn; he became the focus for resistance to the King. Tensions built between the two young men. Each had a large bodyguard, well-drilled, rigorously loyal, and armed to the teeth. Chulalongkorn proclaimed a law against Gatling guns to keep his cousin from acquiring one, but Chulalongkorn's bodyguard had new rapid-fire rifles, and so did Wichaichan's.

One night in December of 1874, a fire broke out in the Palace near the armory and the powder magazine. The guards and slaves rushed to put the fire out, and when the flames had been extinguished, someone noticed that the Second King's men, so close by, had not come to help. Immediately suspicions flared that Wichaichan's men had set the fire.

Chulalongkorn was furious, displaying something of his father's famous temper. He demanded that Wichaichan step down as Second King and accept a ritual purification for the damage done to the King's dignity. Wichaichan lost his nerve. He fled to the British Consulate, which gave him asylum.

The crisis immediately attracted the interest of Thailand's opportunistic and powerful neighbors. British and French ships sailed toward Bangkok. Chulalongkorn saw that he had left himself open to imperialistic intervention; quickly he came down from his former position and offered Wichaichan his job back, but the Second King was thoroughly alarmed and refused to leave the Consulate. Finally, the British governor of the Straits Settlements was invited to come in and mediate the dispute. Wichaichan gave up his army, but remained as Second King.

Chulalongkorn now realized that his abrupt changes had led to this dangerous, ludicrous crisis. His zeal for reform had carried him along too quickly, and the very intensity of his commitment to it had doomed his new government. He withdrew

FOLLOWING PAGE:
With the whole court flat on its face, only Anna dares stand up and meet the King eye-to-eye.

The steamboat docks far up in an isolated mountain camp.

109

most of his program. Power quickly returned to the old ministers.

At the centenary of the founding of Bangkok there were lavish celebrations, but King Chulalongkorn had little to boast about. He had founded his new post office, but his program to abolish slavery had been derailed, and on all sides, Thailand faced new enemies—as the Wichaichan crisis amply proved. The British were still considering taking over the Malay States, south of Thailand, and in Cambodia, the French were challenging Bangkok directly.

In 1882, the French seized Hanoi, and when the Vietnamese Emperor died, a year later, the French took over the entire territory as a protectorate. Since the Vietnamese were Thailand's rivals for Cambodia this brought the French into direct conflict with Chulalongkorn. When in 1886, the British finally seized control over the rest of Burma, Thailand looked like the next target.

But Chulalongkorn had not given up—would never give up, through all the setbacks and the confrontations of his long reign. The Thai colony in London, where many young men were going to

Anna insists on joining the King on his fateful voyage.

OPPOSITE PAGE:
The royal family leaves Bangkok to seek the white elephant–actually, to take refuge from the gathering storm of war.

113

PREVIOUS PAGE:
*On the King's steamboat,
Anna struggles to forgive
the King for ordering
Tuptim's and Balat's
executions. The red flag
with its white elephant
is Mongkut's flag.*

OPPOSITE PAGE:
*King Mongkut brings his
children to the sanctuary
of the monastery in Nong
Khai. Here he prays to
the giant stone Buddha.*

school, and where they were exposed daily to British jingoism, gave him his next opportunity. Frightened by what they saw about to happen to their country, the young Thai in London drew up a detailed plan to ward off the British by installing a constitutional monarchy and reforming the internal government. This would prevent the British and the French from using Thai corruption and backwardness as an excuse to intervene. Boldly, the Young Thai sent their document straight to the King.

Chulalongkorn listened to them. Very courteously he replied that he had not at that time the resources to implement their suggestions, but recognizing deep support for his program, he now began to move again. His first move was to assure the smooth succession of the power of the monarchy. When Wichaichan died, Chulalongkorn left the office of Second King vacant; instead, he announced a new title, that of crown prince, an office of the highest rank modeled on a European form, and appointed his nine-year-old son to fill it.

The old ways were going down. Chulalongkorn, older now, wiser, set in motion a series of reforms. Convinced that a strong defense was Thailand's only chance against the imperialists, he united the country's entire military establishment under the command of his brother, who then modernized the army with new equipment and officer training schools. In 1892 Chulalongkorn moved against the great old families with their entrenched power. He appointed an entirely new cabinet, nine out of twelve of them to be his brothers, other sons of Mongkut, whom he trusted and who shared his views.

But in 1893 the French, smelling weakness in Thailand, created an incident, forced their way into the mouth of the Chao Phraya in spite of Chulalongkorn's prized defenses, and demanded that the Thai accept the Mekong River as their common border. Facing big guns aimed at his capital, Chulalongkorn had no choice but to accept a humiliating defeat. Thailand lost control of vital territory, but more, the Kingdom was shaken to its roots. The French had contemptuously brushed aside the ambitious new Thai military. Chulalongkorn, sick already when the crisis began, became seriously ill and withdrew into seclusion, a depressed and broken man. Public opinion decided that he would die, and wrangling began over who would serve as Regent for the young crown prince.

This was the low point of Chulalongkorn's reign. Yet clearly it was the beginning of his successes as well. The French aggression in Indochina had brought them face-to-face with the British; even while the French were forcing Thailand to give up its claims beyond the Mekong, they and the British were talking about creating a buffer zone between their colonies, to avoid the kind of confrontation that could lead to a major European war.

What they were talking over had already happened. The events of the past century—in particular, Mongkut's maneuverings that kept his country free—had already made Thailand into such a buffer. The English and the French merely agreed on the status quo: a free Thailand—or at least, the core of Thailand, the Chao Phraya Valley and its coastline.

This of course was the heart of Thailand, in more ways than one. Center of Thai culture, the Chao Phraya was also the country's inexhaustible rice bowl, the source of its prosperity, the strength of its economy, and even while the monarchy took its hits, the Thai economy was thriving. Foreign engineers and designers and laborers flocked into the country; they built the first Thai railroad, on which, in 1893, Chulalongkorn traveled, in his first public appearance in months.

The King was recovering. More important, the King had learned. Anna Leonowens had noticed his heroic persistence: Chulalongkorn never gave up, and he always learned from his mistakes. He installed a new defense system, to keep Thailand from the humiliations the French had inflicted, but

Mongkut knows the
future of Siam lies in his
children. He commends
them to the care of
Buddha.

he was now convinced that military power was not
the way to save his country. He came to see that
France and Britain could insult his country because
they were modern states and his was not. He
recruited foreign experts to help him make
Thailand a modern nation. He reorganized his government once again, putting his brothers into all
the positions of power, and driving the great families out. This time, he was not a green boy, and no
foreign power intervened. His reforms succeeded.
By the turn of the century, Chulalongkorn was the
absolute monarch his father and grandfather had
hoped to be: nothing happened in his Kingdom
without his will.

He had modernized Thailand. He had played
the great powers against each other; they had nib-
bled away at the edges of his country, yet its heart-
land remained strong and free. Slavery and the
onerous system of forced labor were abolished. The
tax system had been overhauled and taxes were fair
and fairly collected, and the bureaucracy they
supported was efficient. Bangkok harbor was one
of the busiest in the world. A railroad now chugged
up the long valley of the Chao Phraya. Under
Chulalongkorn the Thai had improved their own
society and imported much that was good from
other societies. Chulalongkorn was, with reason,
one of the most popular monarchs Thailand had
ever known; when he died in 1910, the country lost
an irreplaceable King. Anna Leonowens's star pupil
had fulfilled his promise.

THAILAND'S FANCIFUL WORLD OF MYTH
The Ramakien

*The ascetic Valmiki went to the sage Narada, and
asked, "Is there a man in the world today who is truly
virtuous? Who is there who is might and yet knows
both what is right and how to act upon it? Who
always speaks the truth and holds firmly to his vows?*

"Who exemplifies proper conduct and is kind to all creatures? Who is learned, capable, and a pleasure to behold?

"Who is self-controlled, having subdued his anger? Who is both judicious and free from envy? Who, when his fury is aroused in battle, is feared even by the gods?

"This is what I want to hear, for my desire to know is very strong. Great seer, you must know of such a man."

When Narada, who knew all the three worlds, heard Valmiki's words, he was delighted. "Listen," he replied, and spoke these words:

"The many virtues you have named are hard to find. Let me think a moment, sage, before I speak.

Hear now of a man who has them all.

"His name is Rama. . . ."

So begins the *Ramayana*, the great epic that is loved and told, performed, sung and painted and dreamed all over the Hindu world. Brahminism, the ancient form of Hinduism, reached Thailand long before Buddhism or even the Thai themselves. There, as it does everywhere, the *Ramayana* offers a vision of ideal life, in Rama, the God-King, his faithful wife Sita, and his brother Laksmana, in their battles to defeat Ravana the demon. Even now, where the story is told, parents tell their sons, "Be like Rama!" and their daughters, "Be like Sita!"

The Thai version of the epic is called the *Ramakien*, and was first written down in Ayutthaya, the medieval Kingdom, whose name derives from Ayodhya, Rama's city in the epic. The story was old among the Thai even then. Ramkamheang, great ruler of the first Thai Kingdom, Sukhothai, was named for Rama. All the Kings of the Chakkri dynasty are officially named Rama; Mongkut was Rama IV, and His Majesty the reigning monarch is Rama IX.

The Thai Kings' association with the mythic hero has helped to strengthen and stabilize their dynasty, and they have repaid the great myth with a well-honored cult. The first *Ramakien* was burned up in the conflagration of Ayuthaya, but succeeding Kings undertook the task of reconstituting it. Fostered with such enthusiasm by the dynasty, beloved by the people for its wisdom and variety, the *Ramakien* is everywhere in Thai life, in decorations, in stories and parables, and especially in politics. During Rama I's day, performances that pitted dancers representing him against those representing his brother the Second King sometimes led to bloodshed. In the Thai *Ramakien*, Vishnu is reincarnate as Rama to save the world from disorder and chaos. Small wonder the King wanted to identify himself entirely with the hero.

Yet Rama is everywhere, and his story belongs to everybody.

121

One day when Rama was sitting on a throne, his ring fell off. When it touched the earth, it made a hole in the ground and disappeared into it. His loyal henchman, Hanuman, was at his feet. Rama said to Hanuman, "Look, my ring is lost. Find it for me."

Now Hanuman, who has the shape of a monkey, can enter any hole, no matter how tiny. He had the power to become the smallest of the small and larger than the largest thing. So he took on a tiny form and went down the hole.

He went and went and went and suddenly fell into the netherworld. There were women down there. "Look, a tiny monkey! It's fallen from above!" Then they caught him and placed him on a platter. The King of Spirits, who lives in the netherworld, likes to eat animals. So Hanuman was sent to him as part of his dinner, along with his vegetables. Hanuman sat on the platter, wondering what to do. . . .

When he was finally taken to the King of Spirits, he kept repeating the name of Rama. "Rama . . . Rama . . . Rama . . . "

Then the King of Spirits asked, "Who are you?"

"Hanuman."

"Hanuman? Why have you come here?"

"Rama's ring fell into a hole. I've come to fetch it."

The King looked around and showed him a platter; on it were thousands of rings. There were all Rama's rings. The King brought the platter to Hanuman, set it down, and said, "Pick out your Rama's ring and take it."

They were all exactly the same. "I don't know which one it is," said Hanuman, shaking his head.

The King of Spirits said, "There have been as many Ramas as there are rings on this platter. When you return to earth, you will not find Rama. This incarnation of Rama is now over. Whenever an incarnation of Rama is about to be over, his ring falls down. I collect them and keep them. Now you can go."

So Hanuman left.

Mongkut sees his enemies approaching, and it causes a chill to come over him as if someone had just stepped on his grave.

123

That the country is also staunchly Buddhist, and the King is also a boddhisatva, an enlightened being of Buddha quality, creates no problem. The two traditions have been woven together for centuries. One of the most sacred of Buddhist shrines is the Emerald Buddha, an ancient image of jade which Rama I brought from Vientiane in Laos; painted on the walls of the shrine around the sacred green Buddha are scenes from the *Ramakien*. First made under Rama I, on the fiftieth anniversary of his Chakkri dynasty they were refurbished, and every fifty years thereafter, the reigning monarch has refurbished these murals, the last being His Majesty Rama IX, the reigning King of Thailand, who had the murals refurbished in the 1980s.

The first Chakkri King, Rama I, who supervised the recovery after the flames destroyed Ayutthaya, wrote, "The writing of the *Ramakien* was done in accordance with a traditional tale. It is not of abiding importance; rather, it has been written to be used on celebrative occasions. Those who hear it and see it performed should not be deluded. Rather, they should be mindful of impermanence."

The *Ramayana* has made a permanent thing of impermanence. It is the infinite variety of the tales of Rama that give it such a long life. The tales curl back around each other, sprout up and flower like a great vine. This is the power of the *Ramayana*, to be all things to all the range of cultures of Southeast Asia.

A clever and cultured woman had a doltish husband, whom she tried to interest in culture but could not reach. One day a famous reciter of the Ramayana came to the village. She insisted the husband go to hear the tales told, and he did, but night after night, he sat at the back of the audience and quickly fell asleep.

Finally she took him herself and made him sit by her in the very front, and listen.

The reciter was telling the story then of how Hanuman the monkey had to leap across the ocean to take Rama's ring to Sita his wife. While

Hanuman was leaping across the ocean, the signet fell from his hand and into the ocean.

Hanuman didn't know what to do. While he was wringing his hands, the doltish husband, who was listening rapt in the front row, cried, "I'll help you, Hanuman!" and dove into the ocean, swam to the bottom, and found the signet ring. Swimming up, he brought it back to Hanuman.

Everyone was astonished. They thought this man now was special, blessed by Rama and Hanuman, and thereafter he was treated like one of the wise men of the village, and acted like one, too. Which is what happens when you really listen to a story, especially the Ramayana.

THE LEGACY OF MONGKUT AND CHULALONGKORN
Thailand in the Twentieth Century

The King mounts his horse, ready to rig the bridge at Nong Khai.

Mongkut and Chulalongkorn, between them, brought Thailand into the modern world. In doing so, they ultimately doomed their own way of life. The new values that the Kings championed meant new autonomy for the Thai people; the powerful military they created became a more confident wielder of high authority than the monarchy itself.

In 1910, however, the King was at his peak. Chulalongkorn had created the strongest monarchy in Thai history, staffed entirely by his trusted brothers, and answerable only to him. He died in 1910, of kidney failure, and his son succeeded him as Rama VI. Swiftly the fabric unraveled.

The new King was not a good administrator, nor as farsighted as his father and grandfather. He tried to rule without the help of his uncles and brothers, although his main interests weren't in government at all, but in acting, putting on plays and spectacles, and football games. The ship of state began to drift off course.

World War I started in Europe, and for a while Thailand was neutral, being rather far from the front, but the King decided it would enhance Thai prestige to fight, and he maneuvered the country into the war on the side of the French. But the Thai motorized unit that traveled halfway around the world to strike a blow against the Hun reached the trenches just on time to witness the end of the war.

This seemed to symbolize the country's slow decline: too much show and not enough substance. While the King frittered away his country's resources, trouble was brewing. The army resented the King's special combination of authority and ineffectiveness, and the old guard hated him for shutting them out of the government; even the Queen Mother was shocked at his enthusiasm for acting in stage plays before crowds of ordinary people.

And the world was sinking into the terrible economic crisis that would become the Great Depression, a time of absolute misery for millions of people around the world. Thailand was not immune. Inflation was driving up the cost of living. Many people depended now on city jobs, which could disappear and leave them without means to support themselves—without even the little garden plot of a peasant in the country. The Buddhist *sangha*, whose ethic of compassion and sharing and calm meant so much to the stability of the country, and which provided the main structure for caring for the poor and helpless, was steadily losing ground as more young men went into business than into the monastery. Like so many other societies at the same time, the country seemed to be coming apart at the seams. All around the world, peoples and countries were being swept into a current carrying them on toward economic disaster.

The King died in 1925 without an heir, and his last living brother, the youngest child of Prince Chulalongkorn's seventy-seven children, became King Rama VII. The new King was well-meaning, but did nothing himself, leaving most government

The elephants—like Deli, pictured here—who worked in the film were treated like the natural royalty they are.

129

up to his ministers, as he himself spent more and more of his time out of the country. Unfortunately his uncles and his brothers were no more effective than he was.

Then in 1931, the deepening world economic crisis hit Thailand especially hard. Their money lost its value, and unemployment skyrocketed. The King seemed unable or unwilling to deal with the steadily worsening situation. Finally, a year later, the army moved to overthrow the government. In a bloodless coup, they replaced the absolute monarchy of Rama VII with a constitutional monarchy. The King would remain as the head of state but democratically elected officials would govern the country.

Two main factions dominated this democratic government party: the military and the socialists. Between them there was no real room for the King to operate, and in 1935, after three years of arguing, Rama VII abdicated the throne.

But Thailand wanted its King. Rama VII had no son of his own, and the government

Diagramming chaos—the sketches show the sequence of the explosion of the bridge at Nong Khai. . . as Mongkut's daring gamble pays off.

chose instead the son of another branch of Chulalongkorn's many descendants: Prince Anon Mahidon.

The Prince, however, was only a boy, away at school in Switzerland, and the government was quite content to leave him there. They had a King, but one who did no interfering in the Kingdom, which seemed to suit everybody. Young Rama VIII came to Siam for the first time in his life in 1938, but he left again immediately. The field was open to the democrats and the army.

The army won. In the 1930s, as the world drifted toward open war, Siam militarized rapidly, buying a whole new navy of ships built in Japan and Singapore, a whole fleet of American-made planes. Many in the government looked to Japan as a model for the new Asian nations, a country capable of defying the West and making its own way. In 1933, when Japan made its own way into Manchuria, and the League of Nations condemned the invasion, Siam was the only country that abstained from the vote.

In fact Siam was falling into the Japanese orbit. As in so many countries around the world at this

time, the Thai government had chosen fascism as their destiny. In 1939, the name of the country was changed to Thailand, as part of an effort to build a "cultured" (i.e., fascist) country, one where the government dictated every aspect of the people's lives. By the end of the decade, there were even laws against wearing your shirttail out.

In 1939, France fell to the Nazis. The Thai immediately began to try to recover the territories lost to French aggression in Indochina — Cambodia, Vietnam, and Laos. To do so, they actively sought the support of the Japanese, who strung them along. Then, in 1941, the Japanese launched their full-scale assault on Southeast Asia. To trump the Americans and keep them from retaliating, the Japanese attacked Pearl Harbor; the following day, they overran Thailand. Suddenly the whole world was plunged into a savage war for survival, Thailand in with the rest.

The Japanese occupation stunned the Thai. For centuries they had labored to keep themselves from being colonized by Westerners, only now to fall victim to Asians like themselves. In 1944, they overthrew the puppet government the Japanese installed, and revoked the coerced declarations of war against Japan's enemies. By the fall of Japan, Thailand was on the winning side.

The country was entering a harrowing time. For most of the planet World War II ended in 1945. For Southeast Asia, it continued on for nearly thirty years. First the French, and then the Americans tried to establish control over Indochina, only to lose in long and bloody and tragic struggles that left the area exhausted. Thailand saw no fighting, but much turmoil, and many refugees from the savage struggle in Laos, the violence in Vietnam, and the terrible suffering of Cambodia under the Khmer Rouge. Thailand supported the United States throughout most of the Vietnam War, but as the war ended, drew back from the alliance, and closed American bases.

During this violent era, the army and the demo-

The King, Anna, and their sons enjoy their victory.

133

cratic factions of Thailand struggled for control of the government. Coups followed elections, elections followed coups, in a dizzying spiral of political chaos. The country, desperate for stability, found it in a familiar place: the monarchy.

Rama VIII had lived in Switzerland throughout World War II, but he came back to his country in 1946. There, under mysterious circumstances never satisfactorily explained, he died. His younger brother, nineteen-year-old Bhumipol Adulyadej, another grandson of Chulalongkorn, came to the throne as Rama IX.

The new King was born in Cambridge, Massachusetts, and grew up at school in Switzerland. He finished his studies in Switzerland before he went back to his Kingdom, but on his return to Thailand in 1951 he proved himself a worthy successor of Mongkut and Chulalongkorn. Rather than luxuriate in the panoply of Kingship, he plunged into public service, making the well-being of his people the central theme of his life. Over nearly fifty years he has conducted more than eighteen hundred different projects, including a Thai encyclopedia, ambitious agricultural experiments, hospitals and schools, and canals and dams. He has devoted his entire life to the betterment of his people.

The monarchy personifies the Kingdom of Thailand; it is the country's public soul. The great Kings of Thailand have responded nobly to this duty, dedicating themselves with clear foresight to the furtherance of all their people. His Majesty King Bhumibol's lifelong service to his people proves him truly the wheel-rolling prince at the center of the Thai universe, whose right action keeps the world turning. Through the awful strife of the end of the twentieth century, this longest-reigning of all the world's living monarchs has blended in his person both the past and future of Thailand. In a time of turmoil and fear and convulsive change, he has been the anchor of his society.

In only one way has His Majesty deviated from the path set for him by his illustrious ancestors. He

has one wife, Her Majesty Queen Sirikit. They have four children, a son and three daughters.

Because Thailand was never colonized, the Kingdom escaped the worst of the bloodshed and destruction of Indochina's convulsive liberation from its colonial status. This was largely the work of Mongkut and Chulalongkorn. The two great and wise Kings, welcoming Western ideas, keeping Western imperialism at bay, took their Kingdom on a unique path into the modern world. The story of Anna Leonowens and the King of Siam is a vital record of that event, a piece of living history. Sumptuous and exciting, *Anna and the King* is as wonderful now as it has ever been, an ongoing story of hope for the future, set in one of the most beautiful places on earth, the Kingdom of Thailand, the Kingdom of the Free.

Cecelia Holland is an acclaimed historical novelist known for combining vivid plots, impeccably researched historical backgrounds, and emotionally believable characters. Her latest novels include *Jerusalem*, a tale of the Crusades, which the *New York Times* called "vivid and deeply felt . . . brings as much suspense to political intrigue as to the sprawling battle scenes at which she excels," and *Railroad Schemes*, "a rousing, companionable tale with attractive people, full of dash, thundering hoofbeats, and clattering wheels on new-forged rails" (*Kirkus*). Cecelia lives in northern California.